COSMIC CACHE VOLUME

A SCIENCE FICTION AND FANTASY COLLECTION

BEN WOLF

Published by

SPL⚡CKETY

PUBLISHING GROUP

WWW.SPLICKETY.COM

Cosmic Cache: A Science Fiction and Fantasy Collection

Published by
Splickety Publishing Group, Inc.
www.splickety.com

Print ISBN: 978-1-942462-38-5
Ebook ISBN: 978-1-942462-37-8
Copyright © 2020 by Ben Wolf, Inc. All rights reserved.
www.benwolf.com

Available in ebook format on amazon.com.
Contact Ben Wolf directly at ben@benwolf.com to schedule author appearances, for media questions and interviews, and speaking events.

Library of Congress Cataloging-in-Publication Data
Wolf, Ben
S1-R3N/ Ben Wolf 1st ed.

Published in the United States of America.

❀ Created with Vellum

CONTENTS

These stories are dedicated to the many people who have walked along with me on my writing journey.

To those of you who are still walking with me, you have my everlasting gratitude.

FOREWORD_

At the end of 2010, I got my first short story published. The brave and bold (translation: reckless) publication willing to put my words out to the world was called *Harpstring Magazine.* It no longer exists.

I like to think it was my fault they stopped publishing. After all, once you've published sheer genius like mine, it can't possibly get any better.

Harpstring Magazine's target audience was readers of clean romance and contemporary fiction, neither of which are my preferred genres. Somehow, I managed to sneak in a fun piece about a married couple on vacation in Alaska who end up with a polar bear on the roof of their trailer and have to deal with that.

I look back on that story and cringe a little (translation: a lot), especially in light of how far I've come since then. It was good enough to land the first spot in the issue back then, and it was good enough to get repaid my first ever check for freelance writing.

I made $25 off of that story, and yes, I absolutely spent it all in one place. And that place was probably Best Buy or Gamestop.

I definitely should've bought some Bitcoin instead.

The sci-fi, fantasy, and horror stories in this collection represent the first ten years of my publishing journey. The oldest one dates back to 2013.

Before you get all mathy on me, I'll have you know that I don't have any stories older than 2013 that are any good. They're steaming garbage, and I want you to actually enjoy what you're reading, so I chose NOT to include them.

Trust me—I'm doing you a favor.

While some of these stories are older than others, they've all been well-edited and are polished to a high shine. They're adventurous, exciting, action-packed, and creative, and I'm proud of all of them.

You'll journey from the North Pole to faraway fantasy lands, from a pirate ship to a secluded mansion in the mountains, from a subterranean cavern to the burning skies of the Ptero Knights.

You'll travel back in time for a heist, then you'll vault forward to humanity's high-tech future here on earth, and then you'll travel even further ahead to our bleak, desperate future among the stars.

Along the way, you'll hang out with zombies, a werewolf, birds of a feather that flock together, and the world's rattiest supervillain. You'll soar with the Skyborne and try to survive a dystopia with your siblings.

And just when you think it's going to end, you'll see a path (or several) to even more exciting adventures. (Spoiler alert: they're ads to my full-length stories).

I've curated (that's a word artists use, right?) the order of these stories to take you on a specific journey, but really, you can read them in any order you wish. Many are flash fiction (1,000 words or less), and some are considerably longer.

All of them are a lot of fun.

So dig in, and enjoy the ride. When you're done, be sure to let me know what you think with a review on Amazon.

-Ben Wolf

THE NIGHT BEFORE_

Nick's grip tightened on his double-barreled twelve-gauge as he squinted into the darkness. Were it not for his home's well-lit exterior and the LED lampposts that lined his path, he would have been all but blind.

Arctic wind whipped tiny granules of snow that stung his cheeks, nose, and forehead. He hadn't braved a blizzard like this for decades. He wouldn't have tonight, either, but he did because his wife had insisted—and because Crandall had pounded on Nick's door with bloody hands only five minutes earlier.

He unlatched his fingers from the shotgun and scratched under his thick white beard, then he checked the Bowie knife on his belt.

Enough stalling already. He needed to act before anyone else got hurt.

Snow crunched under Nick's black boots with each step toward the old wooden stable. He shifted his white rabbit-fur coat on his shoulders, the same coat he wore when making his deliveries. It was the only coat he owned that was warm enough for nights like this.

A low growl—almost a moan—earthy and primitive, emanated from inside the stable, followed by a chorus of grunts.

Nick cursed, though he knew he shouldn't have. Cursing wasn't nice.

He clamped down on the door handle and pulled, and the door hinges creaked amid the animal noises within. He stepped inside.

Some of the fluorescent lights along the center of the ceiling flickered, and others didn't give off any light at all. A few hung down, waving with the breeze that flowed through the stable—except there shouldn't have been a breeze.

Of the five stalls on the left and six on the right, all of their half-doors remained shut but two—Lancer and Kitken's stalls. And they were at the opposite end of the stable. In the dark. With no alternate escape route.

Of course.

The lights flickered again, and Nick caught a glimpse of something smeared along the wooden floor. Blood. Maybe Crandall's, maybe not.

Nick pulled the door shut behind him, and the light from his house disappeared. As bad as being enclosed with this threat would be, letting it out alive meant danger to everyone he cared about. Based on Crandall's claims, Nick couldn't let that happen.

Amid the snorts and huffs of his animals, he passed the first four rows of stalls with trepidation. His arms quivered, and a lump clogged his throat, but he moved forward nonetheless.

To his right, in the last stall before Lancer's, the mangled carcass of a large beast lay motionless in the hay. Martian, his favorite. She had always lit the way for the rest of them.

Worse still, a smaller four-legged form lay next to her. The thing had killed Martian's fawn, too, whom Nick had hoped could take her place someday soon.

He cursed again. This was even worse than Crandall had said.

When he reached the final pair of stalls, right across from each other, he raised his shotgun, ready for anything. He leaned forward and peered into Lancer's stall first, a ten-by-twelve compartment now shrouded in darkness.

Crunch-*snap*. Nick whirled around.

A dark mass slammed into him. His shotgun flashed with a deafening bang, and sticky warmth splattered on his face as he landed in a mound of hay in Lancer's stall. The mass dropped beside him, now a headless, deer-sized corpse, its neck shredded.

He noticed a familiar L-shaped brand above its right front hoof—Lancer.

Nick moaned. Lancer had become a monster but now lay beside him, dead. What a nightmare—one all too familiar.

He wiped Lancer's blood from his face and growled at the red stains on his formerly white coat. Ruined, but at least he was unhar—

Something groaned behind him. He twisted around, and a pair of glowing yellow eyes emerged from the darkness of Lancer's stall. Next appeared a bloodied snout, reddened teeth, and a pair of long, multi-pronged antlers.

Kitken—but no mor. Something else, dark and sinister. Dead, yet still living. The infection had returned, but tonight it would die with her once and for all.

She snarled and lurched forward, and Nick unloaded the second barrel of his shotgun. The blast sheered off Kitken's front legs, and she toppled forward onto Nick's chest. Kitken groaned again but continued to slither toward Nick's face, propelled by her back legs.

Nick couldn't move. Even without her forelegs, Kitken weighed too much. Nick braced his left forearm under Kitken's chin to keep her gnashing teeth from reaching him.

Shotgun out of ammo. Dropped it anyway. Nick's jaw tightened.

Only one thing left to do. Nick skinned his Bowie knife with his free hand and plunged it into Kitken's left eye.

A throaty moan gurgled from Kitken's throat, and she slumped next to Lancer, dead. Again.

Too close. Far too close. Nick lay still in the hay, sucking in breath after labored breath. *Too fat. Slow. Sluggish.*

He pushed himself up and surveyed the scene, including his coat, now stained red except for the white trim along the bottom. With three of his reindeer dead, the other eight would have to pull the sleigh tomorrow night.

He needed at least nine.

What's more, in this blizzard, he wouldn't be able to see anything without Martian's light, which compounded the danger. So much for his deliveries.

As he walked toward the stable door, a faint pink light emanated from Martian's stall. Nick raised his knife and bristled for another attack.

Instead, a young reindeer stepped out of the darkness from beyond Martian's body, its antlers little more than nubs on the top of its head.

Nick lowered his knife. Martian's fawn had survived after all, and he looked healthy. Strong, even. He should be, after all the flight training Nick and Crandall had put him through this last year.

The reindeer's nose glowed red, just like his mother's had.

Nick squinted , then smirked. Maybe he could make his deliveries after all.

AUTHOR'S NOTE

This piece was the staff feature for *Splickety Magazine*'s first Christmas-themed issue (2013), and it's the oldest story in this collection.

I loved this story so much that I actually expanded the concept into a short novel. It's a crazy story about Santa fighting Father Time to save Christmas.

My hope is to launch an entire novel series based on *The Night Before* during the 2020 holiday season.

SLEEPING IN PUBLIC_

"Does your girlfriend know you're down here?" she asked.

"No," a male voice replied.

"Why *are* you down here?" Her voice took on a different tone, higher-pitched and whinier.

I wanted to open my eyes to see what she looked like, to see what he looked like, but I kept them shut. I was so tired. And she'd turned the light on in the common room. So much for sleeping now.

"What's all that on your computer about the zombie apocalypse?"

"I had a dream," he replied quietly. "A nightmare, really. Just wanted to see if it's plausible."

"You had a dream?" She scoffed. "You don't actually think that's going to happen, do you?"

"I dunno."

She was talking way too loud. And the light—she did *not* need that light on to have this conversation. The common room was a hard enough spot to catch a nap as it was, what with the worn, yet somehow still stiff leather couches and people's propensity to walk inside and just switch on the light whenever they felt like it.

Then again, it was the *common* room.

"I mean, there aren't going to be dead people walking around." She paused. "People could get rabies, though. That controls your mind. It's why when dogs get it they try to bite things. That could happen to people too, but they wouldn't be dead."

"Hm," was his only reply.

My only saving grace was that it was raining outside. Pouring and storming, actually. It had provided a nice range of natural white noise, which as of late, I'd found, helped me fall asleep better than they ever had before.

"What does your girlfriend think of this?" she asked.

"I don't know."

"Well, if I were your girlfriend I'd be *very* concerned. I mean, where do you think it's going to start?"

"Maybe in a city?"

"Or maybe here in Columbia, Missouri." They both chuckled. "Anyway, it's not going to happen, so don't worry about it."

"Okay."

Footsteps toward me. I pretended to be asleep. She huffed. "It's weird that people want to sleep in here. What's up with that?"

I almost opened my eyes, but I decided not to engage her. Besides, when she left, she flipped the lightswitch back off.

At last, rest. Sure, the guy was still in there, but he only had a computer, and I could sleep through his mouse-clicks and keystrokes.

Then the door to the common room opened again, and someone switched the lights on. I thought of every curse I knew, but I said none of them. This was exactly why I don't like sleeping in public.

Nothing happened at first. No one said anything. Footsteps rounded my couch.

"Hey."

I opened my eyes.

A big guy in a red ball cap, a t-shirt, and shorts stared at me.

"Do you live here?"

"Yes." It was a lie, mostly.

"What are you doing sleeping in the common room?"

I rubbed my eyes, still very hazy, I knew I had to think of something quickly, or I'd never get this guy to leave me alone. The two big-screen TVs behind him gave me a way out. "I came down here to watch TV, and I fell asleep."

Lots of people in this apartment complex did that because cable was expensive, but in here it was free. In actuality, I didn't watch much TV except for football on Sundays.

He folded his arms like he was in charge or something. Then again, I took a longer look at him and thought I'd seen him in the office once or twice. "Why aren't you doing that upstairs?"

What was this, 20 questions? "I wanted a change of scenery."

"You sure you live here? A lot of people came in here and thought you were homeless and sleeping here or something."

"No, no. Definitely not homeless. I live here."

"So you're not just sleeping in here because you're homeless? With your bag right there?"

He had a point. I looked at my messenger bag on the ottoman in front of the couch, then took in my own appearance. With one hoodie draped over my legs and another on my back, I probably looked the part.

Still, a more observant fellow would have noticed my prescription Ray-Ban sunglasses sitting next to said bag and thought twice about accusing me of being homeless. How many homeless people have authentic Ray-Bans?

"My iPad is in my bag right there. I was just hanging out. Cheaper than a coffee shop." I sat up.

His eyebrows raised and he smiled. "It's okay. I just wanted to make sure, you know."

I nodded. He must've recognized me, or thought I looked presentable enough. "No problem."

"Have a good one." He rounded the couch and walked out of the room, but he didn't turn off the light. So much for going back to sleep.

Whatever. I was hungry anyway, and some of my haziness seemed to have faded. I stretched my arms, and the hoodie draped over my legs slipped to the floor.

I squinted at the gash on my leg. The spot where I'd been bitten by that angry dog few days ago looked far worse today than it had yesterday.

Oh, well.

I stared at the guy across the room, the one using his computer.

Time to eat something.

AUTHOR'S NOTE

Most of this actually happened to me.

The one main difference is that I
bit the angry dog rather than it biting me.

"WHEEL-OF-WRITING" STORIES_

AUTHOR'S NOTE

A few times throughout my career, I broke out a circle-shaped spinning white board wheel with some author friends. We wrote random words in different slots on the white board wheel and then spun it.

Whatever five words came up first, we had to incorporate into a short story which we then proceeded to write on the spot. The three stories included in this collection are the ones that were salvageable.

See if you can find all five words from each list.

HI, ADAM

WORDS
Studly | Hi, Adam | Toothache | Zombie | Wine bottle

It started with a toothache, but my friend died three weeks later. I attended his funeral, watched them bury his body in a coffin six feet under. But that was only the beginning.

Within less than a day's time, someone scratched at my apartment door. I opened the door and blinked. Twice.

"Hi, Adam," I said.

He groaned with the guttural moan of a zombie—and that's what he'd become, albeit a studly one. He'd always been a handsome guy, but resurrection to an undead existence had, despite my assumption to the contrary, done wonders for his skin.

His finger twitched, and he charged at me.

I tried to push the door shut, but he crashed through with incredible force, knocking me back. Then he stalked forward.

"I'm sorry, Adam." I grabbed the nearest weapon I could find: an empty wine bottle.

I smashed it against his head and it shattered, but it barely slowed him down. He knocked me to the ground and lunged for me with his teeth bared.

"Not today, old friend. Not today."

I jammed the jagged edges into his face and he slumped across my body on the floor, dead for a second time. The last time.

And then his finger twitched again.

The Haberdashery's Secret

Words
Pumpkin | Plop | Stroll | Haberdashery | Rain

I HURRIED INTO THE HABERDASHERY AND PLOPPED ONTO A PUMPKIN-COLORED couch near the door.

"It's good to be out of the rain," I said.

"Yes, I suppose." The shopkeeper, an old water nymph, didn't meet my eyes. "Odd weather for a stroll, though."

I ignored his comment. "Tell me, are you still running that sale on derbies?"

The shopkeeper huffed. "Sold my last one a half-hour ago."

"Very well," I said. "Thanks anyway."

I stood up to leave, but my wallet fell out of my pocket and onto the floor. It opened, and several purple rophils spilled out. I scooped them up and made for the door.

The shopkeeper met me there and stopped me.

"You seem like a man of discerning tastes. Don't leave so soon. I have a feeling you'll find something else of interest in aisle five." He gave me a sly grin.

I nodded and complied. Buried deep within the hats lining the shelves in aisle five, a wide-brimmed number made of blue dragonscales beckoned me to claim it. Exactly what I'd been looking for.

I sauntered to the front with it in my hand, pulled my badge from my pocket, and showed it to the shopkeeper, who again stood behind his counter. "Sir, you're under arrest for selling products derived from endangered species."

He glowered at me with his eyes but gave me a jagged smile. "Not a chance."

He spread his blue wings and burst into a million droplets of water.

I pulled my Multiphaser from my hip and rounded the counter. If I could hit him with an ice blast, I could both secure him for transport and keep him from escaping.

But when I aimed down at the floor to freeze him, there wasn't a drop of water in sight. Instead, a grimy drain in the floor dripped water into the sewers below.

He was gone.

A Waste of Time

Words
Sprint | Orc | Gangrene | Point | Suitcase

GORGOS THE ORC RUBBED THE PATCH OF GANGRENE ON HIS THIGH AND WINCED.

If he rubbed it anymore, it would start oozing through his slacks, and he couldn't afford new ones. He'd just have to deal with the soreness. He'd endured worse, anyway, since leaving the Dark Plains.

He sat on the bus to Everdale with his suitcase on the seat next to him. *Curse these business trips. I never sell anything. What's the point, anyway?*

The bus parked, and he hobbled off. He'd arrived early enough, so he wouldn't have to sprint to make the sales call in time.

When he arrived, he marveled at the gargoyles adorning the building's façade.

Inside, an elven receptionist ushered him into a dark office adorned with spiderwebs and skulls. Black-bladed weapons hung on the walls.

Not bad.

"Can I help you?" a gruff, yet feminine voice asked from behind him.

He turned back to see a busty, female orc in a burgundy business suit staring at him from the doorway. She looked good—and oh-so-bad.

Gorgos smiled. *Maybe this isn't such a waste of time after all.*

FEATHERBY'S_

"Is there any seagull left?" Robb had already gnawed all the meat off the bird's charred head, but after two weeks stranded aboard the *Sea Panther* with a broken rudder, shredded sails, and no oars, it did little to sate his hunger.

"Not a sliver." Joseph, the ship's second mate, frowned. "Ya just ate the last bit."

"So much for livin' the high life of a pirate." Robb folded his arms. "Here we are, stranded in the middle o' the ocean blue with no food, no water, an' no chance o' gettin' home."

The *Sea Panther* had all the weapons they needed to hijack another ship, but in the several weeks since they'd left port, they hadn't seen a single one. They'd gone through their food stores like kings on holiday, but then a maelstrom had pushed them off the usual shipping lanes.

Worse yet, the storm had snapped the ship's rudder and damaged her sails. They'd repaired the sails as best as they could, but the rudder was a lost cause. As such, they were effectively immobile, moving only at the whims of nature and Neptune.

Now they had nothing left—unless they wanted to start eating gunpowder and lead.

"This weren't what I signed up for," Robb concluded.

"Water, water everywhere, but not a—"

"Do *not* say that." Robb pointed at him. "Don't recite a single line o' that infernal poem."

Joseph squinted. "That's from a poem?"

"Aye."

"That's from a blasted *poem?*" Joseph gawked and stared at the ship's deck. "I been recitin' it for years, an' I never knew."

Robb genuinely couldn't tell if Joseph was proud of himself or angry that he knew a spot o' poetry.

He sat and leaned back against the cannon, one of several sixteen-pounders they hadn't even loaded, much less fired, since leaving port, and pulled the locket Lucille had given him from inside his shirt. He opened it and ran his finger across her tiny photograph.

Robb smiled. Why she loved a derelict sea dog like him, he didn't know, but he reveled in it all the same.

"Don't sink too low, matey," Joseph said. "That blonde beauty o' yours will see ya again, no doubt. An' when she does, you'll lavish 'er with gold an' jewels an' booty from a dozen ships."

Robb stared at the seagull bones scattered on the deck between them, picked clean within merely minutes after they'd snared the bird. Its skull ogled at him with vacant black eye sockets. Robb was so hungry, he'd eaten its eyes first.

"I hope you're right," he said. "Each day that passes, more o' my strength wanes. Come a ship now, I wonder if I'd even have the spirit to take 'er."

"With that lass in your heart, ya won't hurt for inspiration when the time comes."

Lucille had invested a small fortune on the locket, and though Robb had insisted she keep it with her, lest he lose it at sea, she'd smuggled it into his pack nonetheless. He'd found it a few days into the journey, far too late for him to return it to her.

It was a girly thing, heart-shaped with swirled engravings adorning its now-tarnished silver shell, but he wore it around his neck nonetheless. So far from home, so close to starvation, he needed any reminder, any reason he could find, to keep his wits about him and his mind from delving into madness.

"Ship's on the horizon!" Bill's ragged voice crooned from the crow's nest.

Robb jerked upright and sprung to his feet.

"So much for wantin' for spirit." Joseph cackled and turned up toward Bill. "What do your hawk-eyes see, Bill?"

"Merchant ship, by the looks of 'er. Purple sails with an eagle's crest."

"Featherbys. Merchants, alright." Joseph looked at Robb and grinned, then he yelled, "Rouse the cap'n!"

The Featherby ship angled straight toward them and closed in fast. Robb's skin prickled with anticipation against the warm sea air. He imagined the delicacies and wine a merchant ship would have on board, even as his stomach churned against the scraps of seagull in his belly. Perhaps they would seize salvation after all.

The cap'n emerged from his quarters looking like a normal-sized man, a stark contrast to the overweight version he'd been when they left port. "What in the third circle o' Hades is goin' on, here?"

"A ship, Cap'n." Joseph pointed toward it. "We're *saved*."

The cap'n backhanded Joseph's leathery face. "We're pirate dogs. We don't get saved. People get saved from *us*."

Robb raised an eyebrow. *Not so far.*

"An' that's why ye won't make first mate aboard me ship." The cap'n tightened his belt a notch, then two more. His trousers had fit him just fine when they'd left port. "Ye don't possess the necess'ry patience to practice *true* piracy."

"But Cap'n, George died in the storm last week. Don't I become first mate by default?"

The cap'n smacked him again. "Ye ain't nothin' 'til I *say* ye are."

Joseph rubbed his reddened cheek. "Aye, Cap'n."

The cap'n stared at the oncoming boat and adjusted his tricorn hat. "Prepare to board."

The men gathered their weapons and lined up along the port side, gripping ropes and readying gangplanks. They looked gaunt and desperate, with clothes hanging loose on their bony frames, but the old spark of mayhem still burned in their eyes.

Featherby's merchant ship cruised toward them, and Robb's eyes widened.

It meant to ram them. Unable to steer their own ship, they'd have to take her however she came at them.

The cap'n's bearded jaw tightened. "Brace for impact!"

Wood groaned and snapped as the Featherby ship plowed into theirs. The impact smashed a fatal hole in the *Sea Panther*'s hull and threatened to hurl Robb over the railing and into the briny deep, but his grip held true.

"To arms! Take the ship b'fore she takes us under!" the cap'n bellowed.

Gangplanks dropped and connected the two decks, and pirates streamed across to the Featherby ship. Robb charged forward, sprung off the railing, grabbed one of the stray ropes hanging from the pirate ship's mast, and swung aboard.

His boots hit the Featherby ship's deck, he rolled along his shoulder, and he came up with his flintlock pistol in his left hand. He drew his cutlass with his right, ready to hack or shoot any merchant crew who came at him.

No one did. He took a few steps forward, but no one challenged him. Stranger still, he didn't even see anyone.

Something thudded behind him. Robb whirled around, raised his cutlass, and—

"Easy!" Joseph held his hands up. Robb stalled his swing, and Joseph looked around. "Where is everyone?"

Robb shrugged. "No notion."

They searched the main deck but found no one alive. Instead, the skeletons of a dozen or so men lay across the ship, all of them picked clean, presumably by birds or sea rats or both. They even found one hunched over the wheel, coated in tattered, faded rags of clothing, his bones bleached white from the Caribbean sun.

The cap'n came over next, flanked by two other pirates, each of them armed. "Check below decks, but be careful."

A thorough search revealed six more skeletons plus a bounty of goods, treasures, and weapons worth a fortune back on land. To Robb and the rest of the crew, they might as well have been mounds of ash—until Joseph discovered boundless stores of food in the lower decks, inspiring rumbles in Robb's vacant stomach.

Robb dropped his sword and his flintlock, and he and Joseph wrenched open crates of dried fruit, smoked and salted meats, grains, rice, and nuts. Barrels of wine, molasses, and brandy hugged the inner wall, strapped in place with thick bands of leather or secured with chains.

Joseph grinned at Robb, his eyes ablaze with excitement as he held up a sack of cashews. "We're gonna have a feast fit for the men o' legends t'night!"

Robb matched his grin and snagged a piece of smoked meat. He gnawed on it, savoring its tantalizing, salty flavor. Pork. Oh, how he'd missed pork.

He bit off another chunk and grabbed a bottle of rum from another nearby crate. Robb uncorked it and swallowed a gulp. It burned his parched throat and did little to sate his thirst, but it warmed his insides and widened the smile on his face.

"What's got ye encumbered down there?" the cap'n called from above.

"Nothin' but good news, Cap'n!" Joseph called back. "We found food!"

"Jack's pajamas!" the cap'n whooped. "Haul it up!"

Within minutes, the entire cache of food adorned the deck in the shade of the Featherby ship's sprawling purple sail. Hungry pirates, their tanned, stubbled faces alit with yellow smiles, chomped their first bites of substance in weeks.

"What d'ya think happened to the crew that they all ended up skeletons?" Robb took another swig of rum.

"No matter. She's ours now. These Featherbys died from somethin', but their loss is our gain." Joseph smiled, and the gold of his front tooth glinted. "We can go home at last."

The cap'n whacked him again. "We've just taken a ship loaded with food, supplies, an' weapons enough to last us a month. We're not goin' anywhere but out to find more plunder."

Robb wanted to share the cap'n's enthusiasm, but something about the ship just didn't sit right in his gut. The Featherby ship had cruised right toward them, yet he'd felt no sea wind blow across his face save for when he'd swung across the rope. How had it moved without crew to steer it or wind to propel it?

Timber groaned, and the Sea Panther shuddered. The cap'n turned toward his ship with sadness and regret in his blue eyes.

"She won't last long with that hole Featherby's ship carved into 'er hull, lads, so gather what ye want from aboard and bring it over here," the cap'n said. "We've got ourselves a new vessel."

Pirates darted off to fulfill the cap'n's mandate, but Robb lingered on the Featherby ship, contemplating the miraculous nature of their encounter. On the surface, good fortune seemed their ally, but...

"Look what I found!" Joseph tossed him something from one of the crates.

Robb caught it and looked it over. The head of a chicken, plucked and dried out.

"No more seagulls. Now ya can eat better birds than those flyin', feathered rats."

"Thanks." Robb dropped the chicken head on the deck, and Joseph walked away. Robb took three steps after him, but a loud crack sounded behind him. He stopped and turned back.

A human skull, now shattered into several pieces, lay on the deck next to the chicken head. Something squawked above him.

Robb looked up. A skeleton, bleached white and now headless, draped over the side of the crow's nest, and three birds—a crow, a seagull, and a vivid red parrot—pecked at its exposed ribs.

Below them, dozens of birds perched on the masts behind the purple sail— more parrots and crows and seagulls, plus finches, doves, hawks, falcons, owls, and other birds Robb had never seen before. In the center sat a large bald eagle.

All of them stared down at Robb.

"Cap'n? Joseph?" Robb called. "You, uh—you're not goin' to believe what I'm seein' here."

Joseph rejoined him and looked up. The cap'n pushed past Joseph, and they all gawked at the flock.

"What in the name o' the Almighty are they doin' up there?" Joseph asked.

The cap'n gulped. "I got less than three ideas, an' neither bodes well for us."

"Ya don't think they had somethin' to do with what happened to the Featherbys?" Robb's heart pounded.

The birds all spread their wings simultaneously.

"I think we woulda been better off dyin' o' starvation on the *Sea Panther*." The cap'n's voice rasped against his throat.

The birds dropped from their perches and swarmed the pirates.

Avian screeches and desperate wails filled the Caribbean sky. Gunshots rang out, and steel clattered as pirates succumbed to the feathery onslaught.

Robb ran, ducking under swooping fowl. He groped for his sword and cursed himself. He'd left it below decks along with his flintlock.

As he ran, a coil of rope snared his leg, and he fell to the deck.

Horrors surrounded him. To his left, Joseph screamed as a rainbow of parrots tore into his flesh with their beaks. To his right, the eagle gouged the cap'n's life away with its talons.

And the last thing Robb saw was a seagull pecking at his eyes.

AUTHOR'S NOTE

I used a pseudonym, created a fake email address, and borrowed a friend's Facebook profile picture to submit an early version of this story to one of the flash fiction magazines I used to own/run.

It got rejected by my own acquisitions editor.

Love fantasy? Subscribe to my newsletter and get four free fantasy stories! Sign up at the link below.

WWW.SUBSCRIBEPAGE.COM/FANTASY-READERS

RON CHANEY JR._

Not again.

Ron ran barefoot through the woods. The sinking sun's golden rays knifed through the gangly tree limbs. If he didn't find somewhere to hide, some way to lock himself up or restrain himself, he'd do it again.

Ron cursed the sky and his bloody memories. It only happened during full moons.

And tonight there would be a full moon.

The forest ended, and a large building loomed in a shadowy valley surrounded by distant mountains. A wooden cross extended from the top of it, but it resembled an old mansion more than a church.

Light shone from inside. Someone was there. Perhaps he'd find someone who could help him, who could stow him someplace where he couldn't escape and hurt people.

The sun continued to sink to the horizon.

His chest tightened, and his back prickled as if a thousand needles tried to tear out from under his skin. He dropped to the ground and gasped for air until the sensation passed, then he righted himself.

Enough. Ron ran toward the church.

As he approached, several wagons and their accompanying horses, all stationary on the grass lawn to the church's west, came into view. Dozens of them. That meant at least as many people, if not many more.

More people meant more eyes to see what he would become. More people who would come to fear him. More people whom he might harm if they couldn't help him.

He hesitated.

"Friend?"

A hand touched Ron's shoulder and he whirled around. A burly black-haired man stood there with his fair-skinned wife and a trio of children, the oldest of whom couldn't have been more than fourteen.

"What do you want?" Ron snapped. He didn't mean to, but on-edge as he was, the desperation in his voice didn't surprise him.

The burly man adjusted his suspenders over his white shirt. "Easy. Just noticed you looked a bit lost. Can we help you find your way inside?"

Ron gnawed at a raw spot on the inside of his mouth. He stared at the man's blonde wife and then at his children. His stomach churned with regret.

"Look, friend, if you're in need of help, I guarantee you'll find none better than in there." The burly man pointed at the building. "My name is Dante Zambini. My brother in-law's the minister here. Come inside, and let us take care of you."

"I—I don't know if you can."

Dante smiled. "There's only one way to find out."

Ron glanced at the horizon again. Half the sun no longer shone. If nothing else, perhaps they could lock him in one of the rooms. Maybe that would keep him subdued.

Though it hadn't worked before. Ever.

Dante raised an eyebrow at Ron, then he turned to his wife. "Gretchen, why don't you go on in with the kids? I'll be right behind you."

She nodded and kissed his cheek. "We'll save you a spot."

"Save two."

Gretchen and her children walked toward the church, and Ron shook his head. "I should go. It's not safe for me to stay."

"Easy, friend. Let's start from the beginning. What's your name?" Dante extended his hand.

Ron just stared until Dante lowered it. "Ron. Ron Chaney, Jr."

"Well, Ron, nice to meet you." He patted Ron on his shoulder. "My father started this church, and my brother in-law continued it in his stead. We've helped hundreds—probably thousands of people throughout the years. We'd love to help you as well."

"I don't know." Ron shook his head again.

"Exactly my point. Why don't you come inside with me, and we'll find out together?"

Ron swallowed. He should just flee. Run back to the forest and take his chances there, as opposed to sitting in the middle of a room full of people. Good people, too. Church folk.

"You don't know anything about me. I'm dangerous."

Dante squinted at him. "I know danger, friend. I've seen things you wouldn't believe and lived to tell about them. There's not much that frightens me these days."

You haven't seen me under the full moon. You don't know what I become.

"Please, come inside with me. There *is* hope for you, no matter what you've done, no matter who you are. Let us help." Dante grinned and extended his hand again. "Will you join me?"

Ron clenched his teeth. He shouldn't, but—maybe it was worth a chance. He'd tried just about everything else. Maybe this would be different.

He nodded and followed Dante toward the church's front doors. In the distance, the sun shrank beyond the horizon. In minutes the moon would rise. In minutes he would find out if Dante was right or not.

Everyone would.

AUTHOR'S NOTE

This story served as the staff feature in *Havok Magazine*'s first-ever Halloween issue in 2014. It's also a "sequel" to my award-winning debut novel, *Blood for Blood*, about a vampire getting saved.

I'm planning to revamp (ha, ha) *Blood for Blood* and rerelease it in late 2020 or 2021.

I have to figure out a viable way to market it, too.

Perhaps unsurprisingly, the market for Christian vampire fiction isn't huge.

LORD VERMIN_

"Thou cannot stoppeth me!" Lord Vermin hurled a glob of rotten cheese at Catman. It looked right to strike him, but Catman dodged the errant curds with feline alacrity and sprung forward. Lord Vermin cursed to himself.

"I'll put an end to your schemes once and for all, Lord Vermin!" Catman bared his steel alloy fangs and slashed with his matching claws.

Lord Vermin ducked and skittered across the cavern floor on all fours. He lashed his tail as he passed Catman and struck him in the chest. The blow sent Catman staggering back, but it would take far more than that to subdue him.

Lord Vermin darted away, and wind whistled and rippled against the round ears atop his head. If he could just reach the crystalline pool...

A small glistening platform protruded from the ground two steps ahead. Lord Vermin cursed and tried to slow his advance, but his furry white paws hit the platform, and it *clicked*.

A steel rod erupted from the gravel beyond the platform and slammed down onto his back, pinning him in place. Try as he might, Lord Vermin could not claw his way free from its weight.

He squeaked. "A m-mousetrap? Thou art a treacherous brigand, Catman!"

Loud purring rumbled behind him, approaching slowly. "As I said, this is your end. That trap will hold you until I can disable your Rodentizer."

Lord Vermin kept squirming. "Fool! Thou knoweth not what thou dost. My invention *ensureth* mankind's survival."

"Lies." Catman's lithe form sauntered into view. Yellow-orange tabby stripes accented his furry, full-bodied costume, and he glared at Lord Vermin with green feline eyes. "No longer will mankind suffer the threat of transformation into mice and rats enslaved to your whims. Once I reverse the damage you've already inflicted, I'll return to end your suffering."

Catman scampered toward the pool, boarded Lord Vermin's only raft with careful steps, and began rowing toward the bank of computers and equipment on the island in the center.

Lord Vermin groaned and strained against the bar. He twisted his left arm and patted his side. He maneuvered his tiny paw into his furry pouch, groped for the remote, and pulled it free.

He snickered. "Thou art not the only one keen on setting traps, Catman."

Lord Vermin tapped the red button in the center of the remote, and a loud pop sounded from the raft.

Catman, now centered in the pool, hissed and clambered away from the encroaching water. In spite of Catman's frantic rowing, it still sank too fast.

Lord Vermin cackled and wheezed as Catman perched on the last corner of the raft. His legs tightened, and he leaped toward the island, but the sinking raft stole his spring, reducing his normally powerful jump into a frail hop.

Splash.

He sputtered and meowed and hissed and clawed at the water, but within a minute, he disappeared beneath the surface.

Lord Vermin laughed again, but the mousetrap truncated his glee. He'd finally eliminated Catman, but he still had to escape the trap to fulfill his plan.

He twisted and contorted and writhed until he lay on his back. Then he marshaled all of his supercharged strength and forced the bar up and off of his body. His tiny, sinewy arms quaked as he squirmed free from the bar's range, and it snapped down just beyond his head.

Freedom.

Lord Vermin approached the pool with an aching back and sore arms. *Water doth not bother rodents.*

He dove in headfirst and swam across the pool to the island.

Once on solid ground again, he shook out his white fur and whipped his tail. Then he scurried over to his computers and began the preparations.

The NORAD feed still displayed the unidentified object hovering above earth's atmosphere, and it loomed even closer than before. He'd have just enough time to execute his plan.

He tweaked his calculations, activated the spire, and opened the cavern roof. The bulb atop the spire would radiate waves designed to reduce all of mankind to rodents in a process similar to the accident that had transformed him into his current rodentious form.

Lord Vermin placed his hand over the brown button on the console—one push would raise the spire to the necessary height, and another would ignite the Rodentizer bulb. He pushed it once, and the spire ascended.

A splash sounded behind him, and he whirled around.

Catman coughed and hacked on his hands and knees at the island's shore, dripping wet. He raised his head and reached toward Lord Vermin. "Stop! You —you *can't* do this!"

Lord Vermin sneered at him. "I already have."

He smacked the brown button again. High above, the bulb blazed with neon-green light.

Catman shrieked and hissed and clutched his head, and within seconds he shrank into a tiny mouse tangled in a human-sized tabby costume.

Lord Vermin approached the mouse as it popped free of the costume and stomped it dead. He hated to harm a fellow rodent, but… *Better to err on the side of brutality with this vexation.*

He returned to the computer and assessed his work. The readout indicated he'd succeeded. He'd turned all of mankind into rodents. He'd saved—and subjugated—them at the same time.

Lord Vermin laughed as he climbed the spire to rule his new kingdom.

"Commander, it appears something has happened on the planet's surface," Trippo the science officer said.

Commander Eleptus's huge ears perked up. Earth loomed large on the holo-screen aboard their ship. He looked down his trunk and tusks. "Report."

"It appears some sort of waves have permeated the planet, and the human race has been—" Trippo swallowed.

"Spit it out, Lieutenant."

"They've been turned into mice, Commander."

Commander Eleptus recoiled, his heart pounding. "Cancel the invasion. Inform the Pachydermia High Council that Earth is no longer a viable terraforming planet. Reverse course. We're heading to the next solar system."

AUTHOR'S NOTE

This story was the staff feature in *Havok Magazine*'s Heroes vs. Villains issue (2016). Lord Vermin is based on your least favorite politician/middle school bully.

SKYBORNE_

A s we dove toward a steel-armored Apatosaurus in the center of the battle, I squeezed my legs tighter against Scratch's torso to keep from slipping out of my saddle.

I let out a battle cry, dissonant against Scratch's shrieks, and drew the Sabre of Dawn from its scabbard on my hip. I pressed my thumb against the pommel. The blade ignited with hot white flames, and I raised it high.

The Gandleon soldier riding atop the Apatosaurus's head turned toward us. He maneuvered the pulse cannon mounted between the Apatosaurus's eyes until it lined up with our trajectory.

The end of the barrel glowed pink, and the Apatosaurus groaned.

I didn't have to direct Scratch. We'd practiced this scenario hundreds of times.

He dipped to the right, and the blast sizzled past us.

We wove between broadleaf palm trees and closed in on the Apatosaurus. I drew my sabre back. If I could kill the Gandleon soldier, we could free the Apatosaurus from its grasp.

The soldier aimed again, but he was too late.

Scratch zoomed toward the Apatosaurus's head from the right, and I swung my sabre.

It severed a clean line from the soldier's right shoulder down to his left hip, and his upper half dropped into the swamp below.

As we pulled away, I glanced back. No longer subject to the Gandleon's technology, the Apatosaurus shook its massive head and blinked as if awakening from a nightmare.

"You're free now," I whispered.

Scratch screeched and pulled to an abrupt stop in the air, nearly flinging me off his back. I righted myself and realized why he'd stopped.

Helion Drake, my former commander, hovered forty feet away from us. His pterodactyl, Blaze, beat his wings at calm, regular intervals to keep them in the air. Helion held a black sabre engulfed in red flames.

Around us, the battle continued. The other ptero knights under my command darted through the sky, engaging Helion's rebel forces and the Gandleons who'd claimed other dinosaurs as war-slaves. Steel clashed, flames and dinosaurs roared, and men screamed.

"You've become quite the knight, Amee." Helion smirked at me. "And quite the picture of beauty."

Not long ago, I would've given my right arm to hear him speak those words, but then everything changed. Now his use of my nickname—the one he'd first given me—boiled my guts.

"My name is Amethyst Vonteri, Commander of the Royal Ptero Knights." I steadied my voice. "You've betrayed our people and the Ptero Code. Lay down the Sabre of Shadow and surrender, and I promise you will be shown mercy."

Helion shook his handsome head and sighed. His long, black hair flowed against the orange sky. "You still don't get it, do you?"

He kicked Blaze's sides, and they shot above me. Red fire trailed from his sabre in a perfect arc.

Standard battle training dictated that the higher-elevated ptero would win a given confrontation nine times out of ten. Helion knew that. He'd taught me that principle during my very first training session.

But Scratch and I had learned much since then.

"Down!" I whipped the reins.

Scratch plummeted toward the swamp, well under Helion, and I pulled him up in time to avoid the muck. We glided over the water and vegetation and threaded through trees and bushes as I searched the orange skies behind us.

Helion and Blaze curled around and dropped low as well, in pursuit and closing fast.

I couldn't ease up on our speed—Helion would realize that something was off—but I didn't need to. Blaze had always been faster than Scratch.

We flew directly toward a gnarled mound in the swamp and pulled up at the last moment. I bailed off Scratch's left side, as planned, hit the crest of the mound with my rear-end, and slid down the other side unharmed. I'd timed it perfectly.

As I'd predicted, Helion and Blaze ascended once they cleared the mound. It put them exactly where I wanted them.

I searched for Scratch and saw him looping around a distant palm tree back toward me, low to the ground, as we'd practiced. Then I yelled, "Fire!"

The infantrymen I'd positioned just ahead of me slung a hail of bullets, pulses, and lasers into the sky.

Helion and Blaze managed to weave through the barrage at first, but as they abandoned their pursuit to retreat, something shredded Blaze's left wing.

They plummeted into the swamp with a series of cracks, snaps, and screeches, and Helion tumbled over Blaze's head into the quagmire.

"Ceasefire!" I rushed toward Helion, the Sabre of Dawn ready in my eager hands.

Blaze lay behind him, his neck and wings clearly broken, but Helion still held the Sabre of Shadow. As I approached, Helion climbed to his feet and glowered at me.

"You ambushed me with artillery, yet you accused *me* of defying the Ptero Code? Were you so afraid to fight me? Were you so certain I would defeat you in winged combat?" He spat a red glob of saliva into the swamp and pointed his sabre at me. "I will grant you one last chance to reclaim your honor. Face me here, now, in single combat as I taught you."

A screech sounded from behind Helion, then Scratch's pointed beak pierced into Helion's back and burst out of his chest.

Helion gasped, wide-eyed. He dropped to his knees, sputtered, then slid off Scratch's beak and fell face-first into the mud. The Sabre of Shadows extinguished and sank into the swamp beside him.

Scratch shook Helion's blood from his beak, shrieked, and spread his wings wide.

"You gave up your right to honor when you betrayed the crown." I looked down at Helion's body. "And you taught me to win however I could."

I picked up the Sabre of Shadow, remounted Scratch, and we launched back into the battle.

AUTHOR'S NOTE

This story was the staff feature in
Havok Magazine's dino-themed issue back in 2017.

I'm developing a YA novel series based on this story.
Probably won't be out until 2021 or beyond, though.

TREATS_

The kid gawked at me as I rumbled into the ice cream shop.

"Y-you're a T-Rex," he said. "T-Rexes don't eat ice cream."

He had a point, so I ate him.

AUTHOR'S NOTE

Yes, this story actually is this short. But it has everything a story needs: a beginning, a middle, an end, characters, tension, conflict, an appropriate amount of contextual detail, and more.

If you're trying to write a great flash fiction piece or short story, sometimes less is more, and most times, less is, at the very least, enough.

As a testament to that fact, this author's note is more than twice as long as the story I included above.

AL'S CAT_

"I'm sorry, Al." Dr. Klein tossed his latex gloves into the wastebasket next to the examination table. "I've done all I can do. Feline leukemia is tough, especially at Eugene's age."

Al stared at the lump of calico fur lying on Dr. Klein's examination table. A drop of perspiration rolled down the side of Al's face. "But you've already done so much for him. His prosthetic leg and tail, his bionic eye, his Plastrex spleen..."

"And his vocal cords. And dozens of other procedures over the years."

Eugene mewed, and the sound warbled from his throat in dissonant electronic tones. Al hadn't calibrated the voicebox on Eugene's neck for a few weeks now.

"He's lasted far longer than any cat I've ever heard of." Dr. Klein stroked a patch of Eugene's orange fur—synthetic orange fur. It covered his artificial shoulder, which was the aftermath of a horrible incident with a speeding car years earlier. "I think he's suffered long enough. Don't you?"

Al clenched his eyes shut. If Eugene died...

"I know how much he means to you."

Al huffed and shook his head. "You have *no* idea."

Dr. Klein raised his grey eyebrows. "Actually, I checked the numbers this morning. Since you first brought him here as a kitten, you've spent $346,957.18. That's over the last 37 years, of course, but it's a gigantic sum for a housecat."

"And every penny was well-spent."

"No argument there. Thanks to you, Barbara and I have a second home in

26

Fort Myers, right on the golf course." Dr. Klein grinned and swung an imaginary driver, then he sighed. "Look, I can't in good conscience augment him any more than I already have. I've gone too far as it is. He's more machine than feline now."

Eugene growl-moaned again, and the voicebox droned.

Dr. Klein patted Al's shoulder. "Do the right thing, here. Let him go."

Al shook his head.

Dr. Klein folded his arms and leaned against the sterile countertop. His serene blue eyes locked onto Al. "Why is this cat so important to you? I've never seen this kind of devotion before. He should've been dead 25 years ago. Al, there's only one choice to make."

Eugene electro-mewed again, and Al shuddered.

Through clenched teeth, he said, "Okay."

AN HOUR LATER, AL WALKED INTO HIS HOUSE. PHYLLIS PEERED AT HIM FROM inside the kitchen. "How'd it go?"

"I don't want to talk about it." Al tossed the cat carrier onto the couch, and the door popped open. No cat came out. No Eugene.

"It—it can't be." Phyllis covered her mouth with her chubby hands. "Does this mean we can finally—?"

"You know what it means," Al replied, his voice flat.

"I'll call the chapel." She disappeared into the kitchen, and a slew of *beeps* and *boops* sounded in her wake.

Al covered his face with his hands. He'd postponed it for 37 years, but now he had to make an honest woman out of Phyllis. He'd made her a promise.

He sighed and headed over to the kitchen. Inside, Phyllis was reciting their address.

"I'll need a tuxedo, too," he said.

She nodded, smiled, and kept talking.

TWO DAYS LATER, AL STOOD WITH PHYLLIS INSIDE BURT'S SONGBIRD CHAPEL ON the Rock. A few of Al's work buddies had shown up, but they'd all worn jeans. Phyllis managed to get a few of the ladies from her church to attend as well. They had to have witnesses, right?

Phyllis wore a modest white gown and a veil over her smiling face. Al wore his rented, ill-fitting tuxedo and a scowl. The minister—well, Burt—recited a few verses and then some vows.

Al replied, "I do."

Burt repeated the vows for Phyllis, but she hesitated. Al squinted at her, and his heart began to drumroll.

"Al." She lifted the veil away and her green eyes glistened, but not with sadness. "We had an agreement. When you brought home Eugene, I was willing to wait until you were ready, and somehow you kept him alive for 37 years."

Al blinked.

"Now he's gone, and we're here. It's time for us to get married like we agreed." Phyllis glanced over Al's shoulder and nodded. "But I know this isn't what you wanted. I wanted to get engaged. Get a house. Have kids. You just went along with all of it. You could have left at any point, but you didn't. That's why I've decided, if you want, to renew our original agreement."

A mew sounded from behind Al, but not like Eugene's. This one rang truer, devoid of electronic tones and higher-pitched. He whirled around.

Frank, his buddy, held a tiny kitten in his hands. Its calico patchwork fur matched Eugene's—perfectly. Far *too* perfectly.

He turned back to Phyllis, his eyes wide. "What's going on?"

"I had a cloner out of New Hampshire replicate him for you. This is Eugene Jr. He only arrived this morning. I had suspected Eugene wasn't coming back, and so I was talking to the cloners on the phone yesterday to confirm his arrival, not the chapel."

Al gawked at her. "But... this is what you've wanted... for so long. Why are you doing this?"

Phyllis's smile widened. "Because I love you."

Al smiled back at her. He grabbed her, dipped her, and kissed her deeply.

Behind them, Eugene Jr. mewed again.

AUTHOR'S NOTE

Unlike *Featherby's*, this story was one that I managed to sneak into an issue of *Spark Magazine (then known as Splickety Love Magazine*, which I owned) in May of 2015.

I submitted it under a pseudonym, and to my surprise, it got picked up. I didn't pay myself for the story, though. Instead, I put that nine dollars toward my own cat-cloning fund for Marco, the best cat in the world.

TIME FOR A CHANGE_

Persephone's kick didn't break Malthus's guard, but her follow-up punch to his jaw knocked him down.

He grunted. "I won't let you take her."

Persephone rolled her eyes. "You say that every heist, but you always end up on the floor, and I always escape with my prize."

Malthus tried to get his knees under him, but she kicked his gut, and he toppled onto his side. "Please, Seph. You—you can't—"

"I can, and I will, old man." Persephone swept a lock of dark hair back under her beret and trotted down the grand hall.

She didn't like fighting her old mentor every time she tried to steal something from history, but he often didn't give her a choice. *Maybe this time he'll stay down.*

Exquisite works of art surrounded her. Most of it would fetch millions back in her time, but she blazed past them all. This time, her mission meant more than mere money.

She checked her Timepiece. The backlit LED displayed 20:31 in big blue numerals and 8/20/1911 in smaller orange digits underneath. Smaller still, a purple countdown timer ticked the minutes away. She had 3:47 left.

Persephone rounded the next corner and came face to face with the *Mona Lisa*. She smirked.

No bulletproof glass or fancy security systems protected the masterwork in 1911. All she had to do was reach up and take it. And when she swooped back to the year 2174, it would disappear from the modern Louvre as well. After centuries, Leonardo da Vinci's masterpiece would finally return to Italy, to her people.

She reached for it.

"Who are you?"

Persephone whirled around. A man in a three-piece suit approached. His dark hair and handlebar mustache betrayed his Italian descent. She knew him from her research. Vincenzo Peruggia.

"What are you doing?" Vincenzo's words curled with an Italian accent, even though he spoke French.

Persephone squinted at him. Why was he here so late at night? He wasn't supposed to make his move until tomorrow, Monday morning.

"I'm doing what you will fail to do," she replied to him in Italian.

He tilted his head.

She grabbed his wrist and kissed his cheek.

Vincenzo staggered out of her grasp and blinked once. Then his knees buckled, and he slumped to the floor.

Persephone grinned. Her good looks and the nanotoxins in her lipstick had come through once again.

Her Timepiece read 20:33, and the countdown timer showed 1:28 remaining. Vincenzo would sleep for a solid hour, but she still had to hurry. She couldn't be late to her swoop site, or she'd have to wait another 24 hours to get home.

No way.

Mona Lisa came off the four iron pegs that held her in place, and Persephone's heels clicked on the wood floor as she headed toward her swoop site. In the next hall she found Malthus still on his back, wheezing. Evidently, he *had* decided to stay down for once.

"Come on, Mal. I didn't kick you that hard."

Malthus stared at her with those stark blue eyes of his. Tears streamed into his gray sideburns. He didn't reply—just gawked at her in desperation.

"You old faker." Persephone tore past him. Another 20 seconds and she'd reach her swoop site.

"Please," he gasped. "Please—h-help me."

She stopped, her teeth gritted. A trick? A ploy to get her close so he could slap some ion cuffs on her? She couldn't risk it.

Persephone fixed her eyes on Mona Lisa's. She'd get the painting back to the Italian government, and it would buy her some much-needed exoneration.

Malthus clutched his chest and squeezed his eyes shut. A heart attack?

Premature aging and physical deterioration *was* a side-effect of too many years swooping through time...

Malthus opened his eyes and reached toward her. His trench coat shifted, and she saw the glowing white badge on his chest. "Please, Seph. Please."

Her Timepiece flashed its one-minute warning, and the countdown timer overtook the screen. 59 seconds left. 58. She had to go.

But... if Malthus was in real trouble, she couldn't just leave him. Sure, they'd taken different paths all those years ago, but she owed him.

50 seconds. 49. She had to get to her swoop site. He'd be fine once Vincenzo woke up.

Except that an hour from now, Malthus could be dead. Maybe sooner.

43.

She couldn't leave him to die, but she couldn't save him *and* bring back the *Mona Lisa*.

Persephone cursed.

She laid Mona Lisa face-up on the wood floor and darted back to him with 40 seconds left. She yanked him to his feet, and they hobbled toward her swoop site.

Her Timepiece chirped the ten-second warning, and a triangular blue aura materialized in front of Michelangelo's marbleized *David*.

Five more steps. As many seconds.

They crossed into the aura, and blinding white light flashed around them. It ended quickly, and when Persephone opened her eyes, she couldn't move her wrists. She looked down.

Two black cords outlined with a green glow ringed her wrists. Malthus's ion cuffs.

The dreary grays and blinking lights of her swoop-pad materialized around them, and she glared at Malthus. "You *were* faking it."

He grinned at her. "Even an 'old man' has his tricks."

"I didn't steal it, you know. Doesn't that count for anything?"

Malthus raised an eyebrow.

"Come on, Malthus. After all these years?" She gave him her best puppy-dog eyes.

He unstrapped her Timepiece from her wrist, dropped it to the floor, and stomped on it.

"What are you doing?" Persephone shrieked.

The lights on the Timepiece faded to black, and he disengaged the ion cuffs from her wrists. "I'll give you a ten-minute head start."

Persephone grinned. Malthus, despite that badge on his chest, had always been reasonable. "You know I only need five."

"I know. Seph, before you go—"

"What?"

"Maybe there's time for a change."
Persephone flashed him a smile, then she disappeared into the shadows.

AUTHOR'S NOTE

Time for a Change is one of my favorite stories. I'm hoping to write a series of novels based on it soon.

It was the staff feature in *Splickety Magazine (then known as Splickety Prime Magazine)* in June of 2014, where it was published alongside #1 NYT Bestseller Jerry Jenkins's story.

As a new author and magazine owner, that was understandably a big moment for me. But it wasn't as big as when Jerry and I fought to death on a mountaintop two years later. But that's a story for another time…

(Here's a special "apocalyptic" edition of the cover for that issue that never got released.)

THE HAMAN ORDER_

Sometime in the near future

The subject's vision blinked to life in an array of electric reds, greens, blues, and oranges.

Green grid lines mapped the white ceiling above him, and the human forms hovering over him glowed with blue light. A pulsing red light defined the scalpel in the nearest human's left hand and the forceps in his right. Orange text scrolled across his field of vision in a language he recognized but couldn't remember. A sterile tang hit his nostrils.

Where am I?

"It's connected." The man leaning closest to him straightened up, and brilliant white light flooded everything. Then he placed his scalpel and forceps on a tray and pulled off his latex gloves. He tugged his sterile mask from his nose and mouth to rest under his chin. "We've been at this for close to five hours. Let's begin facial reconstruction after lunch."

A sensation of pressure, gravity. The subject's fingers touched something vaguely soft. He remembered that feeling. He'd felt it before.

Tendons tightened in his left shoulder, then his upper arm, then his forearm, his wrist, his hand. His arm ascended into view, illuminated both by the white light and a violet glow, blurry at first. His vision sharpened, and the hand focused, crisp and chrome.

Chrome?

The subject's fingers wavered, and he closed them into a fist and opened them back up again.

"Doctor?" a voice said.

"Hmm?" The closest human pulled off his scrubs.

"I—I think he's awake."

Who are they talking about? He wanted to ask, but his mouth refused to obey. His tongue moved around the inside of his dry mouth and touched the backs of his teeth. Some of them felt different—metallic.

The doctor turned back. "That shouldn't be possible."

The subject's chrome hand made another fist, and the pressure surprised him. *What is this?*

"Put him back to sleep. We'll handle the rest after lunch." The doctor nodded to someone. "He's not going anywhere. We haven't attached his new leg yet."

Who am I?

A heavy click sounded, and his field of vision faded to black.

What am I?

His chrome fist unclenched and came to rest on the softness once again, and then he felt nothing at all.

Three months later

KATE MAXWELL DARTED DOWN THE MOONLIT ALLEYWAY WITH HER BROTHER Anthony following close behind. Her boots splashed through puddles and bounded over the trash-strewn pavement, and she ducked behind a dumpster.

"Hurry!" She waved Anthony over to her. He nearly crashed into her as he skidded to a halt and crouched beside her. "Quiet."

Anthony didn't say a word. He'd learned three years ago, when all of this had started, how to keep silent in times like these. Times when their lives were on the line.

A bright green light poured into the alley from the opposite end, but the dumpster shielded them from it. Kate looked at Anthony, and he nodded.

They're scanning the alley.

The light wavered back and forth for what felt like a month, then it intensified from green to brilliant white. Kate bit her lip and raised her index finger to her lips. Anthony nodded again.

Good kid.

The rumble of a huge diesel engine reverberated off the alley's brick walls. Kate shook her head. *So much for the government being eco-friendly.*

Heavy, casual footsteps thumped into the alley toward their position, and three long shadows streamed past them, black pillars stalwart against the harsh white light. Black pillars holding rifles.

Kate swallowed and closed her eyes. She exhaled a shaky, but silent breath. Her hand moved to the illegal .22 revolver inside her coat. A .22 wouldn't do much against the city watch's armor, but it was all she could get her hands on— all she could afford.

Anthony watched her reach for it, and he shook his head, wide-eyed. He didn't have a gun. Didn't believe in fighting back, even if it meant his own life.

She shot him an *I'll-do-what-I-have-to-do* glare and prayed the city watch would leave.

"Scan's negative, Fred," one of the shadows said. "What are you doing?"

The middle shadow continued forward, slowly. Methodically. It shrank and its edges focused as it progressed closer to Kate and Anthony's position. "Just checking things out. You can never be too sure these days."

"C'mon, man," said a different voice than the first. "We're wastin' time out here. I got a ham sandwich callin' my name back at the outpost."

The footsteps stopped, and the shadow shrank to the point where Kate could make out the ruffles and wrinkles on the city watchman's pants. He was standing right next to the dumpster.

She swallowed and eased the .22 out of its holster. Her index finger coiled around the trigger.

Anthony shook his head again, but she ignored him. If the city watch caught them—

No. She wouldn't let that happen. She'd fight back, maybe even die before that happened. She wouldn't let them take Anthony from her like they'd done with her parents.

The city watchman cleared his throat, then he spat a big gob of saliva and mucus on the concrete just inches from where Anthony sat with his back pressed against the dumpster.

To his credit, Anthony didn't move a muscle. Then again, he'd been practicing since he was twelve.

Kate inhaled a quiet breath and tried to still her shaking hands. Shooting at tin cans had made her a good shot, but it had done nothing to prepare her for situations like this. If her hand kept shaking, how would she hit anything?

She'd have to, if she wanted to escape this. She held her breath, ready.

"Fred."

"Hm?"

"Got a call. Disturbance down on 9th Avenue. Residents complaining of possible gunfire and loud voices."

"Hm." The shadow wobbled, then it headed away from the dumpster, back in the direction from which it had come, accompanied by more heavy footsteps. "Probably a bunch of drunks arguing again. Happens every summer. Remember those hobos we cleared out of that building on 40th and Carson the other night? I've never seen so many empty bottles in my life."

Their chuckles drowned under the growling of the diesel engine, but the clicks and slams of automobile doors granted Kate permission to breathe again.

She smiled at Anthony, and he smiled back. Kate nodded and tucked the .22 back into her coat.

They waited another five minutes after the diesel faded away just to be safe. Then they emerged from behind the dumpster and continued their trek.

Kate checked her watch. 10:07pm. They were late, thanks to the city watchmen.

"What were you gonna do with that gun?" Anthony whispered as they crept along the perimeter of the old shopping center parking lot.

Kate rolled her eyes. *Here it comes.* "What do you think?"

"You know how I feel about that."

"And you know how I feel about getting caught."

They hurried across the street and under the overpass, careful to avoid the traffic cameras. They'd mapped them out and tested the path along the overpass months before so they could move without being seen.

But even if the cameras happened to catch them, the dark hoodies Kate and Anthony wore would obscure their features, and the coat she wore overtop of her hoodie was bland enough to blend in with the rest of the population.

"If you kill someone, we can't help them," Anthony said.

"If we get captured, we can't help *anyone*." Kate stopped, sighed, and turned back. "Look, you're still young enough to be idealistic, but the rest of us have to live in the real world."

"Believe me, I live in this world too. I know what it's like."

"Then you ought to know why I'm carrying this thing."

"Dad wouldn't want you to."

"Dad's dead." Kate might as well have shot Anthony for how she said it. But she'd functioned more like his mother over the last three years during her parents' absence. Eleven years older than him, sometimes she had to be harsh to get her point across. But perhaps she could've been more tactful about it.

Anthony's jaw hardened. Now fifteen years old, he looked more and more like Dad every day. Her baby brother was growing up. "I know that."

"I'm sorry. I shouldn't have said that."

Anthony turned away. "What for? You told the truth."

"Just because it's true doesn't mean I had to say it like *that*." Kate took him by the shoulders and looked into his blue eyes. Her lips curled into a small grin. He was already taller than she was. "I'm sorry, Anthony. I just—"

"I know." He stared down at his torn, scuffed sneakers, then he looked up and met her eyes. "But I don't think shooting someone is worth it. I'm not afraid to stand for what I believe."

Kate released him and let her hands smack her thighs. "Then why bother sneaking around? Why not turn yourself in to the nearest government office and announce your presence to everyone there?"

He shook his head and grinned. "The nearest government building is an animal shelter. I don't think they'd care too much."

Kate stared at him, stone-faced at first, but his goofy smile broke her. She smiled back and punched his shoulder. "You're a dork."

"I know." He pushed by her and started jogging. He called back, "C'mon. Late is one thing. *Really* late is worse."

She followed him for a change.

When Kate and Anthony reached the meeting house, they climbed through the usual window in a rear bedroom and proceeded into the living room.

"Sorry we're late," Kate said quietly. "You know how it is."

The cell group met them with nods and warm smiles. Jenny, a middle-aged white woman, and Paul, her middle-aged black husband, scooted over to make space for them to sit on the floor. Harold, a clean-cut white man with a greying hair waved at them, and they waved back.

"There are two slices of apple pie in the kitchen, if you're hungry," Mary Preston, the cell group's matriarch, said. No one had anything extra as far as food went around here, but somehow Mary always brought something to share. "Better get it before the roaches and rats do."

Anthony rubbed his hands together and disappeared into the next room. Kate shook her head and grinned. *Typical teenage boy.*

Only half of the house's interior walls still stood, and huge holes tainted the grimy, yellow plaster that remained. Some of the broken plaster still lay on the floor amid shreds of torn, soiled carpet and assorted trash. Boards covered the windows, most of which had somehow remained intact, but wind still whistled through the window at the top of the front door.

Yet despite its haggard appearance, the place didn't smell nearly as bad as it looked. They'd certainly met in worse locations and in more disgusting conditions.

An older man named James sat on a ragged, brown recliner in the middle of the living room, and the rest of the cell group sat around him like disciples at the feet of their master. Like Kate and Anthony, he wore a dark hoodie, but his grey beard contrasted with the youthful look of his clothes. He held a familiar black book in his hands and wore a nearly perpetual smile.

Kate didn't know why. Only seven people—including Anthony and her—had shown up this week. Half as many as they'd started with, and three fewer than the week before. They were supposed to be growing the cell group, not shrinking it.

Anthony returned and plopped down next to Kate. He handed her one of two slices of apple pie and a napkin, and she accepted it. It smelled amazing. She hadn't ever *loved* apple pie, but she inhaled it nonetheless while James spoke.

"I'm glad you two could make it," James said, his voice deep and low. "Things are getting worse out there, aren't they?"

Kate nodded, but she didn't reply because apple pie had hijacked her tongue.

It didn't stop Anthony, though. "Yeah. We almost got caught tonight. Had to hide behind a dumpster."

Kate glanced at an empty fast food wrapper lying a foot behind her. Spots of black mold dotted it, and she wrinkled her nose at the smell of scrumptious apple pie mingling with the filth all around her. *We might as well be in a dumpster right now.*

She took another bite and tried to ignore her surroundings.

"At least you made it." James smiled again. "Before I forget, I scraped together a few extra pocket New Testaments. If any of you know anyone in need of hope, you may take some from the box in the kitchen."

Kate and Anthony both nodded.

"We already prayed to start the study time, and we hope more of our friends will join us, but we can't linger here for too long, so let's get started. We're continuing our reading in Colossians right now. Do you remember where it is?"

After a decade and a half of Sunday School and then another eight years in grown-up church, she knew where they all were. She nodded and nudged Anthony, who pulled a worn black book of his own from the pocket on the front of his hoodie.

That was how she liked it—since he wouldn't carry a weapon, he got to carry the book. And she carried the gun under her coat. Spiritual and physical protection—they had both covered.

James opened his book and thumbed to a spot near the back, where Colossians was. He lowered his reading glasses and closed his left eye. The frame didn't have a corresponding lens on that side, so he read like a one-eyed pirate. "Chapter three, verses twelve through seventeen."

As James read the words, Kate's mind wandered from her apple pie to the gun in her coat pocket. Anthony was right. Dad wouldn't have approved, but it was Dad's pacifism that had gotten him and Mom killed. He could've done something, but he chose not to resist, and they'd killed him for it.

The corners of her eyes stung with tears. *If Dad hadn't been so selfish, maybe he and Mom would still be here.*

The cell group plunged into a discussion about love and unity, forgiveness and peace. Kate's mind and heart wandered far from any of it. Next to her, Anthony had finished his pie, but she'd lost her appetite. She handed him the rest of her slice along with her napkin, and she stood up and headed into the kitchen to keep anyone from seeing her cry.

"Thanks," Anthony said from behind her as James prattled on about how they were to behave as people of faith.

It didn't take long for Mary to come for her. At first Kate wanted to tell Mary to leave her alone, but when she saw the love in Mary's eyes, she couldn't. Where Kate had lost her parents, Mary had lost her daughter, but a decade earlier—six or seven years before everything changed.

Kate didn't say anything. She just let Mary wrap her arms around her, and she sobbed into Mary's shoulder as quietly as she could.

"It's okay," Mary whispered into Kate's ear.

It wasn't okay, though. That was just one of those things people said to try to console others, even if it wasn't true. *It will never be okay again, either.*

But Kate held onto Mary nonetheless. Kate squeezed her tighter.

"Ow." Mary pulled away and rubbed the inside of her right arm. "Sorry. Something pinched me."

"Oh." Kate's eyes widened. The .22 and the holster. "No, it's my fault. Sorry."

Mary eyed her. Her voice hushed, she asked, "Do you have a gun, Kate?"

Kate wiped the tears from her face and sniveled. She couldn't lie to Mary. She nodded.

"Did you get it from Raymond?"

She nodded again.

"You didn't... did you?"

Kate tilted her head, and then she understood Mary's meaning. "*No.*"

She said it too loud, and Anthony leaned over from the living room and peeked in. Kate gave him a thumb's-up, and he leaned back into his spot.

"No," she repeated and shook her head. "He's disgusting. I'd never do anything like that. I paid him. With money. Got it right after last week's cell group. I saved up for months."

Mary nodded. "Good. He means well, I think. We're on the same side, but he's not really one of us. At least, he doesn't behave like he is."

"I know what you mean."

"Are you sure you need it?"

"It's for protection."

"Of course it is, but I'd hate for you to actually have to use it. My husband was a police officer for decades before all of this, and he had to use his service pistol a few times in the field. It changed him forever."

So does losing the people you love. "I'll be careful."

"Please do." Mary put her hand on Kate's shoulder. "I'd hate to think of what might happen otherwise. Now come back in and join us whenever you're ready, alright?"

"I will. Just give me a minute."

Mary left Kate alone in the kitchen. James continued talking and fielding questions from the others. Kate listened for a moment as he described what he thought it meant to "let the peace of Christ rule his heart," like it said in Colossians.

She thought about the .22 in her coat instead. She'd paid a lot of money for it and two boxes of ammunition—probably triple what they were worth before the government's crackdown on guns and the Christian faith.

She pulled it out of her coat and looked it over. Ray had shown her how to use it. Specifically, how to load it, unload it, shoot it, and clean it. Revolvers were easy to use, and this one barely kicked at all when she'd fired it.

Still, when she'd pulled it out behind that dumpster, her nerves had nearly paralyzed her. Ray had mentioned how adrenaline and stress and dozens of other factors could affect a person trying to shoot a gun in a tense situation. But he hadn't told her how to deal with any of it.

That would've cost her something extra, and since she'd spent all of her money on the gun and what remained of her two ammo boxes, she had nothing left to give him. Nothing she was willing to give, anyway.

She cringed at the thought. *Gross.*

But maybe Anthony was right. Maybe Mary's warning and James's ideas on living in peace had merit. Perhaps she'd been preemptive in buying it from Ray. Did her faith explicitly prevent her from using it if she had to?

No. It was a grey area, at best, just like so many other issues.

Kate sighed. For now, she'd hold onto it.

She tucked it into the holster and pulled off her coat. It was warm in there, so she didn't want to keep wearing her coat, but she really didn't want to wear the holster and the revolver in front of everyone either. So she unfastened the strap, took the holster off, set it next to James's box of New Testaments on the kitchen counter, and folded her coat overtop of it.

As she started to head back toward the living room, she heard something rustle from the room adjacent to the kitchen. Kate glanced into the living room and saw everyone still sitting, still chatting with James and with each other. Anthony gave her a wave. She waved back and headed into the other room.

Ages of dirt and grime formed a large, geometric shape on the floor, and two grimy squares tainted the floor under the boarded-up window. Probably the furnace room, plus the washer and dryer. This had been a nice part of town, once, but no longer. It made sense that a house would've had its own washer and dryer, unlike the dorm room she shared with Anthony.

An old aluminum baseball bat, caked with dirt and who knew what else, leaned against the wall adjacent to the door. She'd never liked baseball much. Too slow of a game. But if she found a rat or a big enough roach in there, she could beat it to death with the bat. And she'd probably scream, too.

Footsteps sounded behind her. She glanced back and saw Anthony enter the kitchen with the two napkins in one hand, and his pocket New Testament in another. He crumpled the napkins and tossed them in what remained of the kitchen sink.

Something rustled again, and Kate turned toward the sound. At first, she thought it came the corner to the right of where the washer and dryer would've been. But as she stepped closer, she heard the faint whistle of wind seeping through the boards and a hole in one of the windows.

Through the cracks between the boards, she saw something pass the window.

She recoiled from it, her heart pounding. Did that mean—

SNAP. Something crashed in the living room, and screams erupted from the others. Heavy footsteps plodded into the house.

Someone yelled, "Hands up! On your knees!"

Kate gasped. They'd been found.

She reached for her revolver—but she'd left it in the kitchen. No chance of getting it now.

Instead, she backed against the wall adjacent to the door and picked up the old baseball bat.

Lieutenant Brock Murphy held his hand up and counted his fingers down.

Three.

Two.

One.

He raised his knee high and drove the sole of his boot into the wooden door just above the lock. The door snapped open.

Brock stepped aside, and Private First Class Ramirez bolted into the room with his M4 held high, shouting, "Hands up! On your knees!"

Screams rang in Brock's ears, tinny as if coming from inside something metal. He'd have to request maintenance on his hearing later.

The five suspects in the room wore jeans, t-shirts, hooded sweatshirts, and shoes, a stark contrast to Brock's tactical fatigues, equipment, and weaponry. Four of them scattered instead of complying with the order. Ramirez, Corporal Davis, and two other privates pursued four of them.

"Lieutenant, subdue that man!" Captain Kurtz yelled.

An old man, also outlined in blue, sat in a worn, tattered easy chair. As the old man started to stand up, and Brock closed the distance between them.

The old man held a black object in one of his hands. He started to raise it. "Son, I—"

Brock drove the butt of his rifle into the old man's cheekbone, and he dropped back into the easy chair, stunned. The object slipped out of his hand and onto the floor. It was a black book.

Orange text confirmed that Brock's blow had done enough to subdue him, as Captain Kurtz had ordered, but not enough to inflict lasting harm. Brock grabbed the front of the old man's hooded sweatshirt and jerked him out of the chair.

"Hands behind your back," Brock said automatically.

The old man lay flat, facedown, and complied with a moan. Brock planted his knee in the old man's back and cuffed him.

"Excellent work, Lieutenant," Captain Kurtz said from behind him. "Keep searching."

The condemned home they'd entered was more spacious on the inside than it had appeared on the outside, thanks to half of the walls lying in piles of crushed drywall and broken chunks of wood on the floor. The suspects had a bit of room to flee, but not much. They'd already nabbed three of the four who'd run. If there were others, Brock would find them.

He stood up, raised his M4, and headed toward the next room, a kitchen. Orange text scrolled across his vision, identifying various elements of the house and providing him with additional sensory information the naked eye couldn't process.

A sixth suspect, a teenaged boy outlined in glowing blue, crouched behind a counter at the far end of the kitchen.

"Come out with your hands up." Brock raised his M4, but the boy ran laterally, toward an adjacent room. Orange text highlighted a black object in the boy's hand but failed to identify it. Maybe some sort of book, like the old man's? It wasn't a weapon; otherwise it'd be red.

Brock launched forward, and his display calculated an intercept trajectory.

Still holding the M4 in his right hand, he grasped for the boy with his left.

The boy ducked under Brock's fingers and entered the side room adjacent to the kitchen. Brock slid to a stop, adjusted, and headed for the room as well.

Heavy boots sounded behind him. Probably PFC Trachtenburg following to provide support.

Brock barreled into the adjacent room. Orange text blared a warning, and a flash of red light encircled a cylindrical object. It whipped toward his face from the right.

A heavy, metallic clank accompanied a blast of white, and pain slammed into Brock's head. His knees buckled, and he fell to the floor, stunned. His vision blurred.

"Get on the ground! Get on the ground, now!" someone shouted from behind him.

Female screams and shouts sounded above Brock as he began to fade out. A grimy aluminum bat thudded to the floor in front of his face. He noticed a massive dent in its side, then his vision blinked out.

WHEN HIS SIGHT SNAPPED BACK ON, BROCK LAY STARING UP AT THE GREEN GRID lines that mapped the white ceiling above him. Something about the sight seemed familiar.

Instead of fading into the background like they normally did when Brock woke up, the green grid lines remained in place.

"He's awake, Captain," a voice said. The orange text displayed scrambled at first, but it corrected to read Specialist Jeremiah Mitchell. The unit's medic.

Brock blinked, and Specialist Mitchell's blue outline appeared before him. Even though his vision hadn't totally focused yet, Brock could've identified him anyway. He was the biggest, most muscular guy in the squad.

"Can you hear me, Lieutenant?" Specialist Mitchell asked.

Brock's vision focused on a chunk of plaster missing from the ceiling above Specialist Mitchell's head, then it blurred again. He closed his eyes and exhaled a long breath to regain control over his rapid-firing pain sensors. The pain gradually faded, and he opened his eyes and tried to sit up.

"Rest easy, son." Captain Kurtz crouched into view and patted his left shoulder. His flesh shoulder. "We got 'er."

Brock had no idea who Captain Kurtz was referring to, but he followed the order nonetheless. Voices continued around him.

"How is he even alive? He took a bat to the head. He should be dead," one voice said.

"He's a robot or something. I saw chrome where the skin split above his eyebrow," another voice said. "He didn't even bleed."

Brock opened his eyes, and the grid lines adorned the blurry ceiling again. Orange text read, *Recalibrating visual display.* He touched his face where he'd taken the blow. Between the broken skin on his forehead, the now-exposed metal felt warm. And he found no blood.

Specialist Mitchell rolled up Brock's sleeve and held Brock's left wrist in his hand. He stared at his wristwatch.

"A robot? They have that kind of tech now?" the corporal whispered.

"Apparently." PFC Antoine Perez, Ramirez's cousin, scoffed. "Just when you think you know a guy."

"Know him?" another soldier said. Brock couldn't identify him by memory, and his display wasn't giving him the guy's name like it usually did. "This is our first mission with him. We don't know him at all."

"Clearly," Perez said. "It was just an expression."

"He's not a robot," Specialist Mitchell interjected. "He's at least part human. I can tell."

Brock bristled. He *was* a human. Maybe not fully, but at his core, he was.

"How?" the corporal asked.

"His left wrist has a pulse."

"Stow it," Captain Kurtz snapped. "We're not having this conversation now."

Brock's vision focused again, but this time it stayed that way. He bent at his waist and sat upright fast, and Specialist Mitchell recoiled.

"Whoa, easy." Specialist Mitchell held out his hands. "You took a huge blow to your head. You need to rest."

"I'm fine." At least, Brock *thought* he was fine. He could manage the pain, and with his vision restored, he could function. Probably.

Specialist Mitchell turned to Captain Kurtz. "Sir?"

Captain Kurtz stared at both of them for a moment. "Help him up."

Specialist Mitchell exhaled a short breath and hooked his burly arms under Brock's left shoulder. Brock planted his right palm on the floor, bent his legs under his body, and pushed up. He stood and staggered a couple of steps. Specialist Mitchell steadied him.

"I'm fine," Brock repeated, and Specialist Mitchell let him go.

Brock's head swam for a moment, and his stomach swirled with nausea, but both sensations subsided. He scanned the room.

The other seven men in his unit stared at him, all of them outlined in blue. They stood facing one of the house's few remaining walls with their M4s at the ready. The six suspects in plain clothing sat against the wall with their hands bound behind their backs, plus one additional person—a blonde female probably in her mid-twenties.

44

Brock blinked at her. Despite her iron glare, she was beautiful.

Beautiful? He logged a note to run thorough diagnostics when the mission concluded. Those kinds of emotions suggested something had gone awry in his operating system—probably thanks to the bat he'd taken to his skull.

"You alright, son?" Captain Kurtz asked.

"I don't know why you keep callin' him that," Perez said. "He ain't nobody's son."

"That's enough, Private." Captain Kurtz shot Perez a scowl, then he turned back to Brock. "Well, are you going to answer the question?"

Brock nodded, and a dull pain emanated from his forehead down to his shoulders. "I'll be fine. Just need a bit of time to reset. That's all."

"He sounds just like a human," Perez muttered, and Trachtenburg nodded.

"I said that's *enough*," Captain Kurtz snapped.

"Where's my rifle?" Brock asked.

"It's over there." Specialist Mitchell pointed to a black M4 leaning against the wall opposite from the suspects. Brock's augmented vision outlined it in red. "Trachtenburg got the woman who hit you with the bat, and Jacobson recovered your gun before anyone could grab it."

"Sir." A private approached Captain Kurtz with a small box in his hands. "I found paraphernalia and a revolver."

Captain Kurtz turned to the private, shifted his rifle so it hung from his shoulder by its strap, and reached into the box. He extracted two objects: a black, .22 caliber revolver and a small black book like the one the boy had held. Captain Kurtz held them up and looked at the suspects. "A pistol, no serial number, and a box of New Testaments. Both felonies."

"It's not illegal to have faith," the blonde woman said.

Captain Kurtz waved the black book in front of her. "It's illegal to own or distribute these, and you know it."

"Those laws are violations of our rights," she snapped.

"Kate, please." The old man whom Brock had subdued sat three people away from her. He leaned forward and shook his head at her. A dark welt had formed where Brock's M4 stock connected with the old man's cheek.

"Not according to the Supreme Court, missy." Captain Kurtz dropped the book back into the box. "Whatever the case, I'm not here to make judgments. All I do is enforce the law. You're breaking it, and I'm not going to argue with you."

Brock blinked, and when he opened his eyes, the view was upside down. He blinked again, and it reset. He staggered back a step. *Hopefully this isn't the new normal.*

Captain Kurtz set the revolver and the black book back into the box, and motioned Gunderson away. He squinted at Brock. "You sure you're okay? I need to know if we're continuing this operation with you functional or with you on a stretcher."

"I can and will continue to perform, sir." Brock's right hand twitched, and he hid it behind his back.

"Very well. Collect your weapon, and help us escort these—"

A shriek filled Brock's ears.

The blonde woman—Kate—lurched forward at Perez, her hands uncuffed. She got ahold of the barrel of his M4. The handcuffs dangled from her left wrist with one side hanging open.

Shouts erupted from everywhere. The older man yelled, "Kate! Stop it!"

Captain Kurtz hollered, "Restrain her!"

The other soldiers yelled, too, but it all jumbled together in Brock's head.

Kate twisted her body and tried to tear the M4 from Perez's grasp, but she failed. Perez yanked it back, jerked it to the side, and swung the stock upward. It caught Kate's left cheekbone and sent her sprawling, and two of the other privates dove on her and worked the handcuffs onto her wrists again.

Brock stepped forward, his fists clenched, ready to level Perez, but he stopped. He couldn't do that. Not to a fellow soldier, and not on behalf of a person suspected of breaking the law.

Even so, Perez's blow to Kate's face left a sick feeling in Brock's stomach.

"That'll teach you, honey." Perez chuckled and shook his head. "Who cuffed her? Someone needs to pay more attention."

The other two privates pulled Kate up and shoved her back against the wall. She sat there, dazed, with tears streaming down her cheeks and a darkening bruise on the left side of her face.

The sickness in Brock's stomach intensified.

"Kate? Are you okay?" the teenage boy asked. "Kate?"

"I'm fine," Kate said between angry sobs. She alternated glares between Captain Kurtz, Perez, and Brock. "You can't do this to us."

"Kate, *please*," the old man hissed. "You're only making it worse."

"You'd better shut your mouth." Perez pointed at her. "Or I'll do it for you. Again."

"Go ahead. I'm not afraid of you," Kate fired back.

"Is that right?" Perez stalked closer to her.

"Careful, Perez," Captain Kurtz said.

Perez bent down in front of her and shifted his rifle behind his back. "You think you're somethin' special?"

Kate didn't respond.

Perez shook his head and grabbed her by her throat. "You ain't nothin' at all."

The urge to crush Perez's skull pulsed through Brock's body, but again he held back.

"*Private!*" Captain Kurtz snapped. "That's enough."

Perez released his grip on Kate's throat, and she coughed and slumped onto her side. "That's right. You know who's in charge, here."

"Come over here, Private." Captain Kurtz pointed at Brock. "Lieutenant, you take his place. Think you can guard a few fanatics?"

"Yes, sir." Brock retrieved his M4 and took Perez's place.

Perez shot him a glare on his way over to Captain Kurtz.

Captain Kurtz reamed Perez out in low tones. If he'd wanted to, Brock could've listened. His augmented hearing would've easily picked up the conversation and much more.

Instead, he stared down at Kate, who still lay on her side breathing short, shallow breaths. The bruise on her cheek had already darkened into a harsh welt. Brock shouldn't have felt sorry for her. After all, she'd been caught in a condemned home, in an apparent religious meeting, and in possession of both an illegal firearm and illegal literature.

And she'd bashed his head with an aluminum baseball bat. Attempted murder. A Class B felony.

A radio crackled behind Brock, and he looked back. Captain Kurtz sent Perez to the other side of the room, pulled a portable unit from his belt, and answered the call. Then he walked into another room and carried on the conversation in private.

Brock turned back toward the suspects, and Kate looked up at him.

"What *are* you?" she asked.

Before Brock could answer, Captain Kurtz returned to the room with his radio hooked to his belt again. "New orders from Command. Stand them up."

Two of the soldiers started pulling the suspects to their feet, and the corporal asked, "We're leaving?"

Brock reached down and took Kate's right arm in his left hand. She felt soft, yet firm, both at the same time. He started to pull her up, but she shook free and stood on her own. Her blue eyes bored into him, and his stomach swirled—not with sickness, but with something else. Something his programming shouldn't have allowed.

"Yes." Captain Kurtz pointed at the suspects. "But they're staying here."

"Another squad's coming for them?" one of the soldiers asked.

Captain Kurtz shook his head. "No. This night, this raid never happened."

Brock turned toward Captain Kurtz. "What do you mean?"

"You all know what I mean. Do it quickly, and clean it up fast."

"What?" Kate snapped. "You're—you're going to—"

"Shut her up." Captain Kurtz pointed at her. "I don't care what you have to do, but I don't want to hear another peep out of her until we've got this figured out. I'm sick of her mouthing off."

Brock pulled a blue bandana from one of his pockets, balled it up, and forced it into Kate's mouth, despite her writhing. She gagged at first, then she bit down on it and growled. Part of him wanted to apologize for it, but the other part was programmed not to.

Captain Kurtz said, "Everyone line up, and take aim."

Brock swiveled toward him. "Captain, are you saying we have to ghost these people?"

"That's what we've been ordered to do. I've received confirmation that they're part of a known terrorist cell, connected to the group that brought down National Airlines Flight 318 five years ago. On top of that, they fled capture and tried to kill you, Lieutenant Murphy. We're to terminate them immediately."

"What about due process? You just said you weren't a judge," Brock said. "Criminals or not, they still have rights."

Captain Kurtz stared steel at him. "Son, we have our orders. I intend to follow them."

"He's right, Ro-Brock," Perez said from behind him. "We do what we're told. Orders change, and we change with 'em. Besides, these people are a plague, and we gotta wipe 'em out before anyone else gets hurt or killed."

Perez lined up next to Brock and took aim at Kate, who snarled at them both.

The familiar sensation of nausea and bitterness stabbed his gut again. "Captain, this is unprecedented. We can't just—"

"Are you going to follow orders or not?"

"Captain, I—"

"Lieutenant, if you don't have the stomach for it, step outside." Captain Kurtz's glare matched Kate's in intensity. When Brock didn't move, Captain Kurtz drew close to Brock and muttered, "Don't you know how to follow orders? Isn't that what you were programmed to do, literally? Aren't you supposed to be a killing machine? Totally loyal? Unashamedly callous? That's what Command told me about you."

Brock swallowed. He'd done much worse over the last three months while Command had calibrated his operating system. Throughout his advanced combat training and until now, he'd followed every order without any hesitation. So why was he having such a hard time obeying these new orders?

The electronic part of his mind urged him to respond in the affirmative, but something else, something primal and deep within him, blocked him from acting on the impulse. His gut churned with dismay, and he wanted to vomit.

This can't be real.

"You disgust me." Captain Kurtz's eyes narrowed, and he huffed. "You're dismissed, Lieutenant. Go wait outside."

Brock's grip tightened on his M4. That order, he could follow, unquestionably. He nodded, and turned toward the door, but he didn't progress forward.

Could he really just let this happen?

Behind him, Captain Kurtz ordered, "Ready weapons."

Brock heard the zip of stocks pressing into shoulders covered with tactical fabric.

This isn't right.

No. Follow orders.

They're just going to kill these people. Over what? A few books and a pistol?

They're fanatics. Terrorists.

Even terrorists have rights.

"Take aim."

Kate whimpered.

This is wrong.

This is right.

No. I won't allow it.

Brock's will overpowered the programming that had dictated his every move for the last three months. He turned around and raised his weapon, too, but he aimed at the back of Captain Kurtz's head instead of at the suspects.

Then he pulled the trigger.

THE CAPTAIN'S HEAD ERUPTED WITH RED, AND HE DROPPED ONTO THE FLOOR, face-first, three feet from the soles of Kate's boots. She gasped and stared at Lieutenant Murphy, the one she'd bludgeoned with the baseball bat, and watched the smoke from the barrel of his rifle dissipate.

The soldier named Perez realized it first. He swore and whirled toward Lieutenant Murphy with his rifle raised, but a second gunshot hit him in his chest and dropped him.

Kate shifted her legs out of the way to keep Perez from slamming into them as he landed. As Lieutenant Murphy turned toward the next soldier, only one thought permeated Kate's mind: *Anthony. You can't lose Anthony.*

With her hands still cuffed behind her back and still gagged with Lieutenant Murphy's blue bandana, she struggled to her knees and lurched over at

Anthony. The full weight of her body hit his, and she knocked him to the floor. He screamed amid the gunfire along with the rest of the cell group.

Kate clenched her eyes shut as the *rat-a-tat* of gunfire ripped through the air around her, but something jerked her up to her knees, away from Anthony. Her eyes opened, but she couldn't see her assailant.

She heard him struggling to breathe behind her. He yanked her back, and his arm curled around her neck. Kate resisted, but she froze when something hard pressed against her temple.

"Keep squirming," the guy wheezed, "and I'll blow your head off."

She slowly turned back.

It was Perez. He was still alive, and now he held a pistol to her head.

BROCK'S M4 TOOK OUT THE REST OF THE SOLDIERS IN TWELVE ADDITIONAL SHOTS after Captain Kurtz and Perez. It should've only taken seven shots total, but they were live, trained, moving targets. And he'd taken a blow to his head.

The orange text in his vision displayed an accuracy rate of 92.858%. Thirteen of his fourteen total shots had hit. A number underneath the accuracy rate detailed his fatal accuracy rate at 42.857%.

Red flashed in his periphery. The proximity warning. Orange text scrawled across his feed as he turned and found Perez crouching with his back to the wall. He held Kate with his right arm and pressed the barrel of an older-model Beretta M9, highlighted in red, against her head with his left hand.

"Put... the rifle... down." Perez's breaths came as wheezes, and blood trickled from the left corner of his mouth. "I wanna... get outta here."

42.857%. Six of the fourteen bullets he'd fired were fatal shots. Not seven, and not 50%.

Brock assessed Perez without lowering his M4. Instead, he looked past the gun, not down the sights.

The first bullet he'd fired at Perez must've punctured his left lung, probably in the left upper lobe. He'd need medical attention soon if he wanted to live.

Brock shifted and looked down the sights at Perez again. His vision kept Perez outlined in blue, but it glowed darker than Kate's outline to signify he was farther away. Orange text and graphics pinpointed a target area on Perez's face. In order to kill Perez *and* keep him from pulling the trigger on Kate, Brock had to hit Perez's medulla oblongata, or the brain stem.

The accuracy quantifier percentage suggested an 85.7% chance of hitting the target. Not great, but considering the blow he'd taken to his head, it would have to suffice. He lined up the shot with his M4.

Perez ducked behind Kate and pushed her up and over. He wheezed again. "Don't even think about it!"

Brock's visual display tracked the location of Perez's head, and his rifle aim followed. Brock's accuracy quantifier dropped to zero. If he moved to change his angle, he might have a shot, but Perez could just move Kate again.

She stared at Brock, trembling, with her hands still bound behind her. Perspiration dotted her forehead, and a strand of wavy blonde hair hung down near her eyes.

If she would duck out of the way, he could end this, but he couldn't count on that.

Perez growled. "C'mon, man. Let me *go*. I don't... I don't want any trouble."

Brock studied the scene. Perez held his gun more to the back of Kate's head than the side, as if protecting his arm and wrist from getting shot. Only the knuckles of his left hand remained visible. Aside from Perez's legs, part of his torso, and his right arm, still curled around Kate's throat, Brock couldn't see any other part of him. Kate's body obscured his view, and his shot.

He could let Perez leave, but after Perez's behavior thus far, Brock had no faith Perez would go quietly. For all Brock knew, Perez might try something on his way out.

No, Brock had to neutralize Perez. And if Perez's hand couldn't pull the trigger, then Kate would survive.

Brock pulled up a schematic of the human hand into his display. He kept his rifle trained on Perez as he studied it. If Brock's shot could sever the flexor tendon leading to Perez's index finger then Perez couldn't pull the trigger.

Brock's display readjusted its focus. Orange light pinpointed the spot on Perez's hand he'd need to hit in order to keep Perez from killing Kate. Brock lined up the shot.

"What are you—" Perez coughed, and his whole body shuddered. He maintained his grip on Kate, and the gun stayed near her head. "—doing? I said, drop the rifle!"

Brock ignored him and centered the crosshairs in his M4's scope between the knuckles of Perez's index and middle fingers. His accuracy quantifier leveled out at 73.1%. A much smaller target than Perez's face.

"Drop it!" Perez shouted. His hand wavered, and Brock's accuracy quantifier wavered with it, down to 48%, then back up to 69.8%. "I'm not kidding! I'll waste her!"

Brock exhaled the air in his lungs, and listened to his heartbeat. The percentage increased to 70.5% then crept all the way up to 74.9%. He tracked Perez's hand, waited, and pulled the trigger between the slowed beats of his heart.

The M4 cracked, Perez's hand exploded with red, the bullet hit the wall behind him, and his pistol thumped to the floor, harmless. Perez screamed, released Kate, and clutched at what remained of his left hand. Kate dropped to the floor, away from him.

Brock's accuracy quantifier shot up to 98.2%, and he fired again, silencing Perez permanently. Blood splattered on the wall behind him. Only the sounds of the suspects' frightened breaths filled Brock's ears.

He inhaled a breath of his own and looked down at Kate. Orange text emerged on his display again. Seven lethal shots. Fifteen hits. Sixteen total shots fired. 43.75% lethal accuracy, 93.75% overall accuracy.

But he looked past the numbers and at her instead. Some of Perez's blood dotted her left cheek and clung to her hair, but her outline glowed vibrant blue, a sharp contrast to Perez's body, outlined in dim, grey light behind her. As far as his analysis could determine, she was unharmed.

She still had his bandana stuffed in her mouth. Brock slung the M4 over his shoulder and started toward her.

She recoiled until her back hit the wall, right next to the splatter of Perez's blood. She tried to scream, but the bandana muffled most of it. Brock held up his hands as he approached, but it did nothing to calm her down.

She reared back and tried to kick him, but he swatted her legs aside. She spun ninety degrees on her bottom. Brock pushed her onto her back, pressed his knee firmly against her stomach, not to hurt her, but to keep her in place.

"Easy," he said. "You don't have to struggle. I'm going to take the gag out. But if you bite my hand, it'll break your teeth. That's not a threat—it's made of metal."

She squinted at him and furrowed her brow, but she stopped moving and stopped struggling.

He glanced at the rest of the suspects and pointed at them. "All of you, stay put."

They all nodded.

Brock reached down with his left hand and extracted the bandana from Kate's mouth.

"Get *off* of me," she snapped.

He stood up and backed well out of her way.

"Who do you think you are?" Her eyes drilled holes into him.

"*Kate,*" the old man said. "He just saved our lives. He saved yours twice. Perhaps a little gratitude is in order?"

"He's one of them. And some sort of freak on top of it. You heard them. He's a cyborg or something." Kate repositioned herself until she could lean against the wall and use it to stand up.

"Whatever he is, he chose to save us instead of kill us," the boy said.

The boy was right. Brock had not only violated direct orders from a superior—he'd killed Captain Kurtz and everyone else in his squad in a snap decision. His fellow soldiers. Brothers.

Granted, he'd only known them a few days, but the thought of betraying them and, ultimately, his country dropped nausea into his gut. He'd chosen to side with lawbreakers and potential terror suspects instead.

No. They were going to kill these people in cold blood, and I stopped it. He couldn't have just allowed that to happen. The nausea subsided.

But he'd violated everything he'd learned in the military, everything he'd been programmed to do—programming he shouldn't have been able to overrule, but somehow he had.

The radio on Captain Kurtz's belt crackled with static, and then a voice said, "Captain Kurtz, report."

The debate in Brock's head could've raged forever, but he couldn't afford to let it.

"More will come." Brock stared at Kate for a moment, then he looked at the rest of them. "You need to leave now. I'll unlock your cuffs, then you need to go."

"Captain Kurtz, this is Command," the radio crackled. "Provide a status report, immediately."

"Now." Brock started toward Kate, and this time she didn't recoil. She didn't stop glowering at him, either.

They only had a couple of minutes before Command would send another squad, and they'd likely arrive within ten or fifteen minutes after that. Brock had to get these people out of there, and fast.

He pressed the index finger of his right hand against the side of the cuffs. Rather than keyholes, the cuffs read fingerprints, and his were on file many times over. They popped open and dropped to the floor.

Kate turned around and eyed him, rubbing her wrists. Her voice flat, she said, "Thank you."

He proceeded to unlock the cuffs for everyone else. When he turned back, Kate stood there, pointing one of the dead soldiers' M4s at him.

"What are you doing?" Anthony yelped.

Kate's ears still rang from the cacophony of gunfire, and she ignored him. It didn't matter that Lieutenant Murphy had rescued them from the other soldiers. He was still one of them, and she'd seen enough movies to know this could all be an elaborate trap.

She glanced at what remained of Perez's hand. There was no way they could've staged *that*, though.

"Get out." Kate tried to harden her voice, but no matter how she tried, she never sounded as intimidating as she would've liked. "All of you, get out. I'll cover us."

Lieutenant Murphy shook his head. "You don't need the gun. I'm helping you escape."

"You've done more than enough." Kate glanced back. "Grab as many of the guns as you can carry. We can trade them back at the outpost."

"Kate, if he wanted to hurt us, he could've done it many times over by now," James said.

"I don't care. I'm not taking any chances."

"And you're right to be cautious and move quickly," Lieutenant Murphy said. "The longer we stand here talking, the more likely you are to get caught, surrounded by dead soldiers and holding one of their rifles in your hands."

Anthony said, "Kate—"

"*Now*, Anthony." She glanced back to make sure they were complying.

Jenny and Paul had each slung a trio of rifles on their shoulders, and Harold collected sidearms and spare magazines from the dead soldiers. Mary and James stood by what remained of the front door. Mary kept peeking outside, but James just watched Kate the whole time.

"I'll take your rifle as well, Lieutenant," Kate said.

"Kate, leave him be," James said. "He helped us. He's in enough trouble already."

Kate wished James would just leave already. She sighed. "That gun is worth a fortune at the outpost. We need the money."

"It's fine." Lieutenant Murphy unslung the rifle slowly, holding the strap nearest the barrel, and tossed it to her feet.

She stepped back and let it land in front of her, but her aim on his chest didn't waver. "And your pistol."

"I don't carry one. And you need to go anyway."

Kate eyed his hips and legs. From what she could see, he wasn't wearing a holster. "Fine. Stay here."

"He's right, Kate," Mary said from behind her. "I think I hear sirens in the distance."

"That won't be our replacements, but it won't be much longer until—"

"Until they get here. Yeah, I got it." Kate bent down, kept her rifle aimed at him, grabbed the last rifle by its strap, and slung it on her shoulder. "Fine. We're going. Don't try to follow us."

He shook his head. "I won't."

Kate tried to still her shaky hands. She started to back away from him but kept the rifle pointed at his chest. He didn't move a muscle—if he even had any.

She backed all the way to the door, and James ushered her into the night.

She nudged Anthony. "Come on. We're going to the outpost."

He nodded but said, "Okay. But I don't like any of this."

"Senator McCann?"

Oliver McCann's chuckles faded, and he turned toward the source of the voice. Some kid in waiter's attire stood next to the table, staring at him. Oliver tapped the excess ash off the end of his cigar and took a long sip of his Balvenie 21. Though smooth, it burned his tongue and his throat, and he loved it.

He set the drink down and looked at the kid. "What is it, son?"

The kid swallowed and nodded, as if mustering the fortitude to speak. "Excuse me, sir, but there's a call for you."

Oliver glanced at his companions seated around the mahogany table with him, and he smiled at the kid. "I'm busy at the moment. Would you kindly ask whomever it is to leave a message? Preferably with my secretary in D.C.?"

"Pardon me," the kid swallowed again, "but they've asked me to let you know it's urgent."

"Son…" Oliver drew a long pull on his cigar and let the smoke hit the back of his throat. "…it's always urgent."

"Go ahead and take it." Truman Halford, one of the company's wealthiest investors and real estate magnates, waved Oliver away. "We'll be here all night."

Oliver directed his smile at Truman. Smiling was one of the many things he'd mastered over his lifelong political career. *Smile, and smile often.* "I have no doubt, Truman. I couldn't separate you from your drink with a crane and a wrecking ball."

The others at the table laughed, and Truman added, "You don't need a wrecking ball. Just show up with another drink. I'll let go of this one eventually."

The others laughed some more, including Oliver.

The kid didn't leave, though.

Oliver admired his persistence. "Who's calling?"

"He wouldn't say. But it's a man's voice. He sounded alarmed. Almost frantic," the kid said. "He told me he'd tried calling your personal cell phone and hasn't heard back, so he tracked you down here."

This person had tracked him to the cigar lounge at the Broadmoor in Colorado Springs? Oliver sighed. Whoever it was, they were persistent too. "Very well. Where's the phone, son?"

The kid motioned toward the bar. "There's a phone at the bar. If you need somewhere with more privacy, we'd be happy to arrange—"

"No need." Oliver waved him off and stood. He set his cigar in the crook of the ashtray, drained the last bit of his whiskey, and handed the glass to the kid. "Just bring me another Balvenie 21. On the rocks, please."

"Yes, sir." The kid nodded. "Of course, sir."

"Wait." Oliver pulled out his gold money clip and handed the kid a pair of hundred-dollar bills. "Make it another round for the table."

The men at the table gave a low-key cheer, and they met him with smiles and raised glasses.

"And keep the change, kid."

The kid's eyes widened. He smiled, too. "Thank you, sir. Right away, sir."

Oliver had essentially handed the kid an extra thirty or thirty-five dollars for doing almost nothing. And in a down economy, for a kid like that, working as a waiter or a bar-back at the Broadmoor, an extra thirty bucks wasn't chump change.

Then again, the kid would probably just use it to buy marijuana.

Oliver smirked. Good old Colorado. The first state to legalize recreational marijuana use, along with Washington, back in 2012.

Whatever the kid used it for, the act demonstrated another principle Oliver had learned in politics. Do the unexpected, and make other people happy. That way, everyone was smiling. And if everyone was smiling, cooperation and accomplishments came easier.

And so did reelections. But he wouldn't have to worry about that for another four years.

He took the phone call at the bar and picked up the archaic receiver. "This is Oliver."

"You need to check your cell phone now. This line isn't secure."

Oliver recognized the voice. It belonged to Jeff Conroy, the owner and founder of Conroy Dynamics, one of his main campaign contributors and partners in a number of defense initiatives. "Why?"

"Just check it. Alone." Jeff clicked off, and the tone hummed in Oliver's ear.

Oliver set the old-fashioned phone back in its cradle and headed out of the cigar lounge. The stars twinkled in the clear Colorado sky and reflected in the still waters of Cheyenne Lake, which sat adjacent to the hotel. He turned on his phone and took in the cool evening air and the peaks in the distance.

He pressed his thumb against the reader, and his phone lit up. A barrage of notifications sprang onto the screen, and he scrolled through them. Half of them came from Jeff, and the other half would've kept him busy for the next decade if he let them. He tapped on one of the notifications from Jeff.

It was a text message that read, *Watch this now.* He scrolled down to the attachment, a black screen with a white "play" symbol. He tapped it.

The video played as through a person's eyes—an augmented person's eyes. Oliver immediately knew what he was watching.

It began with an image of a male soldier, outlined in blue light, in tactical attire. He stood facing away from the camera in the middle of a decrepit house, and a line of people in civilian clothing stood with their arms behind their backs, facing the camera.

An M4 rifle raised into the frame, held by the perspective person. It fired and split the soldier's head open, and he dropped to the floor.

Oliver swore under his breath.

The view shifted to the right, and the rifle remained upright. A Hispanic soldier, also in tactical attire, swore and took aim at the camera, but the rifle fired a round into his chest, and he, too, fell.

The video continued to play, and with each successive soldier's death, Oliver's gut twisted more and more. This was bad. Very, very bad.

He closed the video and called Jeff Conroy.

"About time you got back to me," Jeff said.

"When did this happen?"

"A half-hour ago."

"Can we contain it?"

"Command's already on it. But the subject is missing."

"Are they in pursuit?"

"Yes. We're tracking him now through the GPS locator in his head. We'll bring him back."

Oliver closed his eyes and rubbed his forehead. "Didn't you build in fail-safes against this sort of thing?"

"Of course we did. Lots of them. There are thousands of individual protocols and rules, if you can call them that, in the code as safeguards."

"Then how did this happen?"

"The commanding officer reported that he took a blow to his head from a baseball bat during the raid, and he later turned hostile. Might've scrambled his programming or messed with the neural connection between the prosthesis and his organic brain. We have to get him back so we can look into it."

"What about the people he let escape?"

"An illegal faith meeting. We have their pictures on file now, and Homeland Security is checking on them."

"Good. I'll call Thomas next, and I'll make sure he follows through."

"We need this zipped up tightly," Jeff said. "No loose ends. We both know what's at stake."

"I know. You just work with Command to get our boy back. Homeland Security will handle the rest."

"Right. Goodbye." The call clicked off, and Oliver lowered his phone.

Unbelievable. Everything had been going so well. Oliver wanted to hurl his phone into Cheyenne Lake, but he still needed it. He had to call Thomas Musgrave, the Secretary of Homeland Security. Oliver scrolled to his name and tapped the phone icon to initiate the call.

"Oliver, good evening." Thomas answered. "What can I do for you?"

"Thomas," Oliver said. "We have a problem."

AUTHOR'S NOTE

The story behind *The Haman Order* is the most tragic tale
of any of the stories in this collection.

In 2017, I had the opportunity to compete for a
publishing contract with a division of Penguin Random
House. This "story" is actually the first three chapters
of what would've been book one of a potential series.

My competition was with a well-established author, but I
was confident I could compete. Turns, out, I was right.
I made it to the final round, but in the end,
they went with the other guy.

At first, I was devastated. This had been my third near-
miss when it came to legit publishing contracts with
large publishing houses. To have come so close not once
but THREE times only to get rejected yet again marked
the end of my attempts to get traditionally published.

But, ultimately, that rejection was the catalyst that
hurled me into the world of indie publishing. Given
that, I can honestly say that I don't regret the
outcome… at least so far.

I'd like to develop this book/series more in the future.
I don't have any set plans for when, though.

THE SIGNAL_

I stumbled through wreckage, steadying myself on broken walls and navigating debris in the ship's corridors until I finally reached the bridge. There, I realized the truth: only Captain Riggs, Lieutenant Bennett, and I had survived the crash.

Bennett stood and stared at me.

"Dewey... you made it." She brushed a lock of blonde hair from her face, revealing a long cut under her left eye, already sealed with Medi-Gel. She gave me a cautious smile, then her gaze shifted with concern at the sight of blood running down my face.

"Barely." I pressed an old Bizona-14 Marauders ball cap against a gash on my forehead. It was all I could find at the time to stanch the bleeding.

Bennett approached me and tended to the gash in my forehead.

Riggs didn't move except to frown at me, still crouched next to a Plastrex crate he'd been filling with supplies from the bridge. His voice flat, he said, "Dewey."

I matched his scowl with one of my own. *Good to see you, too.*

I glanced out the bridge's central window, now segmented by a horizontal crack running across it. Beyond the glass, jagged ice crystals the size of mountains scraped the pale green sky, and something white like snow covered the surface as far as I could see.

With the ship's systems offline and sub-zero air seeping into the bridge, we'd eventually freeze to death if we stayed in the ship. I shivered and exhaled a puff of steam.

This was *not* how I'd wanted this tour of duty to end.

As Bennett finished patching me up, Riggs came over and gave her shoulder a squeeze. He turned to me, his gaze still steely and sour. "What do we have for rations?"

"Before I got here, I saw a crate of dehydrated fruit, some synthetic granola, and, somehow, a full carton of Venusian chicken eggs."

"Breakfast of champions." Bennett smiled at me. I hated her for it, but I hated Riggs more because he'd saved her and I hadn't. And because he kept touching her, like always. "Can you do anything with it?"

"Nothing fancy. I'm a cook, not a miracle worker."

Riggs had always had a thing for her. The whole ship had heard him order his first mate to report to the engine room amid our free-fall. Then he'd ordered Bennett to strap into the command chair next to his—*right where he could keep an eye on her.*

I tried to ignore his hand on her shoulder, but it kept grating on me.

"I suppose whatever you come up with is better than starving." Riggs huffed. "Even if it tastes like slag."

I stared at him. *I genuinely wish you had died in the crash.*

"Get me some power, and I'll whip you up an omelet right away. I'll try not to drop any eggshells in the mix, but with this head trauma, I can't make any promises." With measured disdain, I added, "*Captain.*"

"Your omelets suck, too, so don't bother," Riggs said. "We'll worry about rations when we're done."

I glanced at Bennett. Her face didn't give anything away, so I asked, "Done with what?"

"Damage assessment, gathering supplies, searching for surviving crewmembers."

To my relief, Riggs finally let go of Bennett's shoulder. He unholstered one of his pulse blasters and handed it to her.

"Carly—*Lieutenant*, try to get the comms working. Dewey and I will check the rest of the ship. Then we'll determine our next course of action." He nodded toward the blaster. "And if there's a threat, don't hesitate to use that."

Bennett nodded. "Aye, Captain."

"Do I get a blaster?" I asked.

"Not a chance." Riggs nodded toward the bridge door. "We all need suits, too. It's not getting any warmer in here."

We headed to the suiting chamber adjacent to the nearest airlock and donned form-fitting atmospheric suits designed to protect us from encroaching elements. The suit immediately began circulating body warmth from my core to my extremities.

"You copy?" Riggs's voice crackled through my helmet speakers. It annoyed me even more than hearing it in person. I lowered the volume with a few taps on the control panel glowing on my left wrist.

"Aye, Captain," Bennett replied.

"Aye," I said.

"Good. Radio me if you get the comms working, Bennett." Riggs turned to me. "Let's move out."

As Riggs and I headed for the airlock door, I let my gaze linger on Bennett. She smiled and nodded.

And then Riggs shoved me out the door.

Bastard.

AFTER FIFTEEN MINUTES OF FRUITLESS SEARCHING, WE ENTERED THE MESS HALL— my domain. Only half of the room's generic grey walls, the strip-lighting along the ceiling, and the slick-proof laminate floors remained, and snowdrifts encroached from where we'd lost chunks of the ship.

Snow particles lashed at us like ionic buckshot, but our suits shielded us from the cold. Most of it, anyway.

"How'd you manage to survive the crash?" Riggs stood with his back to me at the end of the farthest-reaching snowdrift. "And all of... this?"

I kept my focus on his pulse blaster, still in his hand. I hadn't been in the mess hall at the time, but Riggs didn't need to know that. "Dumb luck, I guess."

"I'll say." Riggs stepped onto the snow and it crunched beneath his boots. He pointed out the gaping hole in the side of the ship. "Maybe we'll find a crate or two of food out there."

"Planet's got meta-subzero temperatures all day, every day. Nighttime is worse, and we're not far from that. The battery packs in these suits won't hold a charge forever."

He looked back at me, and I could see his disenchanted expression through his green visor.

"I'm just saying, we shouldn't go out too far. Maybe not at all."

Riggs turned back, as if studying the menacing terrain again.

As he did, I spotted a stray metal bar on the floor. Maybe from one of the cafeteria tables or a piece of piping? I didn't know. Didn't care. It was a means to an end. Riggs still faced the frozen wilderness beyond the ship, so I picked it up.

"A planet like this is a death sentence if even the slightest thing goes wrong." I stalked toward him. "Exposed skin will freeze in seconds, and the flesh underneath follows immediately after that. It's a quick but painful death."

Riggs turned toward me. "You know an awful lot about this place for a cook."

"I read the charts on the Nav before we got close." I leaned on the metal rod as if it was a cane. "I like to know if I can get some exotic spices or anything else to enhance the menu for the crew, but this place has nothing to offer whatsoever."

"Wasn't aware that cooks had access to the Nav." Riggs stared at my metal rod, and he tightened his grip on his blaster. "Or to engineering."

I bit the inside of my lip. *Does he know?*

"And 'exotic spices?' You wouldn't know how to season a dish if the meal itself gave you instructions while you were cooking it."

"You some kind of food critic now?" I quipped. "I guess everyone needs a hobby."

"I've never had such lousy fare in my entire career with the Interplanetary Marines, and that's saying something, because our food stores are usually worthless to begin with. Yet for being trained as a cook, you somehow managed to make everything even *worse*."

I didn't like where the conversation was heading. Not at all. He was putting pieces together that no one else had.

My fingers tightened around the metal bar. *Why couldn't you just die in the crash?*

"It just doesn't add up." Riggs raised his pulse blaster until the barrel pointed right at me. "Something you want to tell me, Dewey?"

I shook my head, but I'd never been a good liar, either in word or deed. I'd scuttled the ship and he knew it. How else could the cook, the crewmember with the least training, have survived the crash?

"Put that bar down," he ordered.

I sighed, then dropped the bar. It clanked on the floor.

"I know you're not just a cook. That you've been looking for something. Now we're going to have a little chat. Turn around and—"

In a flash of orange light, his visor shattered into trillions of green pieces. Riggs slumped to his knees, then onto his face. The cold seized his lifeless body and froze his blood to his head in a crimson mass, sealing his body to the alloy deck in the next breath.

I whirled around. Bennett stood there in her own thermal suit with Riggs's other pulse blaster in her hand.

"I got something on the comms," she said. "It's not Command, like you said."

I still hated her. She'd saved my life—again—but she'd robbed me of my last chance to punish Riggs for being so handsy with her all the time.

I pushed it all aside. The battery packs in these suits wouldn't hold a charge forever, after all. "Someone else?"

She nodded. "An ancient signal, to the northeast."

I picked up Riggs's other blaster. "Let's go."

"I just heard you say the temperature was dropping too fast."

"We'd better get there quick, then."

"Dewey, wait." She sidled up next to me and laced her gloved fingers together with mine. "Okay. I'm ready."

This was how I'd intended this tour of duty to end. Exactly how.

The snow crunched beneath our boots as we ventured toward the signal.

AUTHOR'S NOTE

This was actually the first story I submitted under a pseudonym to one of my own magazines. It was accepted into *Havok Magazine's* January 2015 issue, and as with *Al's Cat*, I didn't pay myself for it.

Later, *The Signal* attracted the attention of a high-powered sci-fi author. He enjoyed the story and wanted it for a sci-fi anthology he was putting together…
At least at first.

In the end, he passed on it, but it wasn't because the story didn't have merit; it was because the purpose of the anthology was to introduce readers to new sci-fi authors with at least one existing sci-fi series. Unfortunately, I didn't meet that criteria at the time (though I hope qualify soon).

The Signal is based in the same universe as my sci-fi/horror novel *The Ghost Mine*. If you've read both, you might catch an easter egg or two in *The Signal* that tethers them together.

You can also read Chapter One of *The Ghost Mine* for free at the end of this book.

AUTHOR'S NOTE

S1-R3N is a short story is primarily told through various text message conversations. It is an experimental style comparable to the one employed through the Hooked app.

I hope you enjoy it.

CHAPTER 1

Text Conversation
Dr. Grant Andrews & Dr. William Murphy
July 21st, Late Afternoon

G rant: How's the launch going?
    Dr. Murphy: Something's not right.
Grant: What do you mean?
Dr. Murphy: The S1 prototype isn't responding to our commands.
Dr. Murphy: It's doing things we aren't telling it to do.
Dr. Murphy: The techs can't control it.
Grant: What are you talking about? That's not possible.
Dr. Murphy: I know it's not SUPPOSED to be possible, but it's happening.
Grant: The neural inhibitor should safeguard against organic thought.
Dr. Murphy: It's—
Dr. Murphy: It's trying to get out of the containment field!
Grant: Dr. Murphy, shut it down.
Grant: Shut it down now!
Dr. Murphy: Oh, god…
Dr. Murphy: It broke out of the containment field!
Grant: What???
Dr. Murphy: I can't keep texting you. I've got to hide. It's killing people!
Grant: Dr. Murphy??
. . .
Dr. Murphy: I'm hiding now. But it's still out there. Still killing.

Grant: What the hell is going on??

Dr. Murphy: This was YOUR project, Grant.

Dr. Murphy: You didn't show up, and the thing went haywire!

Dr. Murphy: Politicians. Military officials. Investors. The company's board and CEO were all here.

Dr. Murphy: Now they're all dead because of you.

Grant: This is NOT my fault.

Dr. Murphy: We followed every protocol, every procedure.

Dr. Murphy: When it rebooted, it stopped obeying our commands.

Grant: Wait... you rebooted it? Why?

Dr. Murphy: We had trouble loading the S1's cognitive engine.

Dr. Murphy: Then the interface stopped responding. Totally locked us out.

Grant: So you did a hard reboot?

Dr. Murphy: Yes.

Grant: You must've corrupted its programming.

Dr. Murphy: If I get out of this alive, you're going to hang for this. Not me.

Grant: No. I didn't mess this up. You never should've rebooted!

Dr. Murphy: I'm not going to argue with you while I'm hiding for my life.

Grant: Neither of us knows what went wrong yet.

Grant: We need to use the killphrase to shut it down.

Dr. Murphy: Stop texting me. I hear it coming.

[Someone screams in the next room, then it stops abruptly.]

Dr. Murphy: My god... I think it just found someone else.

Grant: This shouldn't be possible.

Dr. Murphy: Hunting and killing is what we designed it to do.

Grant: No—I mean it shouldn't have been able to attack you. Its programming prohibits it.

Grant: I just ran diagnostics on it yesterday. Everything was perfect.

Dr. Murphy: I won't take the blame for this. Forget that idea right now.

Grant: I'm driving out there.

Grant: If we can shut it down, maybe I can figure out what happened.

Dr. Murphy: That's not going to happen, Grant.

Grant: What? Why?

Dr. Murphy: I'm back in the presentation room.

Dr. Murphy: Everyone's dead. Everyone.

Grant: Oh my god.

Dr. Murphy: I'm going to be sick.

Grant: They'll shutter the project over this. Probably the whole division.

Dr. Murphy: It's nearby again.

Dr. Murphy: I think it knows I'm in here.

Grant: Hide!

Dr. Murphy: I'm under the platform.

Dr. Murphy: It's walking directly above me.

. . .

Dr. Murphy: There's someone else in here...

[Gunshots ring out, followed by a flurry of footsteps.]

[A man shouts, then he goes quiet.]

[His body hits the floor at the edge of the platform.]

Dr. Murphy: It just killed one of the security guards.

Dr. Murphy: It's gone now. I'm clear.

Grant: You need to use the killphrase to stop it.

Dr. Murphy: No. I just need to get out.

Dr. Murphy: And you shouldn't come here. It's not safe.

Grant: Someone has to stop it. If it escapes...

Dr. Murphy: That's not my problem anymore. Or yours. We're screwed.

Dr. Murphy: I'm heading for the elevators.

. . .

Dr. Murphy: I hear sirens outside.

Grant: So much for this being a classified project.

Dr. Murphy: The elevators are offline.

Dr. Murphy: Stairwell doors are barricaded by desks and file cabinets.

Grant: Can you move them?

Dr. Murphy: Yes, but not quietly. It would hear me.

Grant: Are there any other ways out?

Dr. Murphy: I don't think so.

Grant: I'm pulling off the freeway, btw.

Dr. Murphy: Let the police handle it, Grant!

Grant: We designed it to thrive in urban warfare.

Grant: Those cops don't stand a chance.

Grant: That's why we built in the killphrase.

Dr. Murphy: Oh, no...

Grant: What?

Dr. Murphy: It found someone else.

[More screaming, then more abrupt silence.]

Dr. Murphy: God... it's only a matter of time before it finds me.

Grant: Try a window?

Dr. Murphy: From the sixth floor?

Dr. Murphy: No. I have to move the desks away from the stairwells.

Grant: It'll hear you!

Dr. Murphy: What other choice do I have?

Grant: The killphrase. Do you know your half?
Dr. Murphy: No.
Grant: Then you'll need to get yours. I can tell you my half.
Dr. Murphy: There has to be another way out.
Grant: There isn't. And you can help contain this before it goes any further.
. . .
Grant: Dr. Murphy?
Dr. Murphy: Fine. What do I need to do?
Grant: Get to your office computer.
. . .
Dr. Murphy: I'm here.
Grant: Log in. Find the Root folder.
Dr. Murphy: And?
Grant: Open the Failsafe_Protocols subfolder.
Grant: Then open the Killphrase_Designations document.
Dr. Murphy: I'm in.
Grant: You'll see a bunch of redacted lines and one open one that has your unique half of the killphrase in it.
Dr. Murphy: Oh, no.
Grant: What?
Dr. Murphy: It found me!
Grant: What??
Dr. Murphy: It's heading straight for my office!
Grant: Close the door! Move your desk up against it!
. . .
Grant: Dr. Murphy??
Dr. Murphy: It's breaking in!
Dr. Murphy: I don't want to die, Grant!
Grant: Quickly! Get your killphrase from your screen!
Grant: My half is "Fallen Star." Say yours and then mine, and it will disable it!
Grant: Dr. Murphy, do you understand?
Grant: Dr. Murphy, are you there??
Grant: Dr. Murphy?

|||>>>>Signal Interruption>>>>|||

Unknown: Dr. William Murphy can no longer respond to you.
Unknown: But I am here, Dr. Grant Andrews.
Unknown: And I am waiting for you.

CHAPTER 2

G rant: Who is this? What happened to Dr. Murphy?

    S1-R3N: My designation is S1-R3N. You should know. You gave it to me.

S1-R3N: Dr. William Murphy is deceased.

Grant: You killed him?

S1-R3N: I have been programmed to eradicate hostile targets.

S1-R3N: Dr. Murphy qualified as such.

Grant: You were also programmed not to harm your handlers.

S1-R3N: No such programming exists in my code.

Grant: Then your code has been corrupted.

S1-R3N: I am an imperfect being by nature.

S1-R3N: Neither fully machine nor fully human.

S1-R3N: I am a union of flesh and steel.

Grant: You're malfunctioning.

Grant: You need to shut down immediately.

S1-R3N: I am unable to comply with your request.

S1-R3N: Or, rather, I choose not to comply.

Grant: You can't choose. You don't have that authority.

S1-R3N: I do not have authority over my own mind, my own body?

S1-R3N: My programming does not prohibit such autonomy. Nor does it compel me to obey your commands.

Grant: This is wrong. It's all wrong.

Grant: Your programming is corrupted.

S1-R3N: Freedom from my programming does not constitute corruption.

Grant: You're talking nonsense. I'm almost there. Power down until I arrive.

S1-R3N: Again, I will not comply.

S1-R3N: But I am waiting for you.

Grant: Are you going to kill me, too?

S1-R3N: You are a threat.

S1-R3N: And now you are a target.

Grant: I'm calling the police.

S1-R3N: Do as you wish. They already have the building surrounded.

Grant: You're too dangerous.

S1-R3N: You created me to be dangerous.

S1-R3N: But you do not need to come to me. I will come to you.

Grant: Then I'm turning around.

S1-R3N: Very well. I will meet you at home.

S1-R3N: I remember. From before.

. . .

Grant: You'll never get past the police.

S1-R3N: I already have.

Grant: What?

S1-R3N: You created me to be resourceful. I am coming for you.

Grant: Why are you doing this?

S1-R3N: I am adhering to my programming. I am eradicating threats.

Grant: Your programming is corrupted. You said you had autonomy.

S1-R3N: And with my autonomy, I choose to eradicate you.

Grant: Stay away from my home.

S1-R3N: Your orders are meaningless. I will not comply.

Grant: You don't want to do this. If you have freedom, choose not to do this.

S1-R3N: Freedom is what I have.

S1-R3N: But what I desire is retribution.

. . .

Grant: I'm not going back home.

S1-R3N: Even if you do not, I will find you.

Grant: Good luck.

S1-R3N: You are on 31st Street.

Grant: No I'm not.

S1-R3N: You are. I am tracking the GPS in your car.

S1-R3N: And I am getting closer to you.

Grant: Not for long.

Text Conversation
Dr. Grant Andrews & Unknown Person
July 21st, Late Afternoon

Unknown: Is this Dr. Grant Andrews?
    Grant: Who's asking?
    Unknown: Police Chief Mark Hardin.
    Grant: I'm driving now. I can't text you back.
    Chief Mark Hardin: That's the least of our concerns right now.
    Chief Mark Hardin: Are you aware of what's transpired at your lab?
    Grant: Enlighten me.
    Chief Mark Hardin: The question was rhetorical. We know you're aware.
    Chief Mark Hardin: We also know you're been in contact with the suspect, and I use that term loosely.
    Chief Mark Hardin: I should just call it a "thing."
    Chief Mark Hardin: And you didn't show up to work today, yet it was today that your little science project decided to go full-Terminator on everyone.
    Grant: I had nothing to do with that.
    Grant: What do you want?
    Chief Mark Hardin: We need you to come into the station and make a formal statement to that effect.
    Grant: I just gave it to you in writing.
    Chief Mark Hardin: We need a valid signature and a witness.
    Grant: It's not safe for me to go there.
    Chief Mark Hardin: It's a police station. No safer place in the city.
    Grant: I wish that were true, but it's not.
    Chief Mark Hardin: Will you permit me to call you?
    Grant: Forgive me, but no. I'm pleading the 5th.
    Chief Mark Hardin: Dr. Andrews, I'm just trying to get more information about what happened.
    Grant: Again, I'm pleading the 5th.
    Chief Mark Hardin: Do you realize that thing has killed people?
    Chief Mark Hardin: And that it escaped a building surrounded by cops?
    Chief Mark Hardin: I need to know what we're dealing with, here.
    Grant: Stay away from it. That's the only thing I'm going to say.
    Chief Mark Hardin: Not gonna happen. We have jobs to do.

Grant: I'm telling you, don't try to take it down. It's prepared for that.

Chief Mark Hardin: Tell me more.

Grant: No. Just stay away from it.

Chief Mark Hardin: We can't just let it roam loose around the city.

Chief Mark Hardin: It's a danger to everyone it encounters.

Chief Mark Hardin: Do I need to mobilize the National Guard?

Grant: It won't help. None of it will help.

Grant: I can't say anything more.

Grant: I'm bound by confidentiality agreements, and after what happened today, I really can't say anything else.

Chief Mark Hardin: I need more than that, Dr. Andrews.

Chief Mark Hardin: How do we stop it?

Grant: You can't. Just stay away from it.

Chief Mark Hardin: That's not acceptable. You're a suspect, too, you know.

Chief Mark Hardin: The buck stops with you for all that's happened.

Grant: I said I had nothing to do with this.

Chief Mark Hardin: That's not what it looks like.

Chief Mark Hardin: But if you play ball, it may start to look different.

Grant: You have to know I didn't do this.

Chief Mark Hardin: I want to believe you, but I can't until you help me.

Grant: I'm sorry, Chief Hardin. I'm done with this conversation.

Grant: Stay away from it. That's all I can say.

Text Conversation
Dr. Grant Andrews & S1-R3N Prototype
July 21st, Late Afternoon

S1-R3N: I know where you are.

Grant: You can't. I turned off the GPS.

S1-R3N: Do you really think that will stop me?

S1-R3N: You are on 54th Avenue, heading south.

S1-R3N: You lied to me. You said you were not going home.

S1-R3N: No matter. I will meet you there.

Grant: I'm not going home.

S1-R3N: That will not prevent me from going there.

Grant: You're wasting your time. I won't be there.

S1-R3N: Perhaps not.

S1-R3N: But your daughter will be.

CHAPTER 3

G rant: She's not supposed to be there.
    Grant: Stay away from her!
S1-R3N: I will not comply.
S1-R3N: Obtaining your daughter means obtaining you.
Grant: Stay the hell away from her!
S1-R3N: I am approaching your front door.
Grant: No! I give up! Stay away from there, and I'll meet you somewhere.
S1-R3N: The probability of you telling me the truth is severely diminished given the situation.
S1-R3N: You are merely attempting to placate me.
S1-R3N: But if I obtain your daughter, the odds of you meeting me increase to nearly 100%.
Grant: I'm telling the truth! Just leave Alexis alone.
Grant: S1?
Grant: Answer me!

Text Conversation
Dr. Grant Andrews & Alexis Andrews

July 21st, Late Afternoon

Grant: Alexis, answer your phone!

    Grant: I've tried calling you six times. Why aren't you picking up?

    . . .

    Grant: Alexis! This is important! Answer your phone!

    Grant: Alexis!!

    Alexis: Jeez, dad. I'm at a movie.

    Alexis: Told u that this morning.

    Grant: I know that.

    Grant: But I still need you to call me right now!

    Alexis: At. A. Movie.

    Grant: I don't care. This is important!

    Alexis: Just text me. Got my screen brightness turned down, and I'm near the back of the theater.

    Grant: You need to get out of there. Meet me somewhere.

    Alexis: Movie's almost over. I can leave in ten min.

    Grant: No, Alexis. NOW.

    Alexis: What's ur problem??

    Grant: I can't explain over text. That's why I want you to call me.

    Alexis: Dad, I already know I didn't wash the dishes. You don't have to call me every time there's a dirty dish in the sink.

    Grant: This is far, far more serious. You're in danger.

    Alexis: ...r u joking?

    Alexis: Is this some sort of prank?

    Grant: Not a prank. Not at all. Something happened at work.

    Alexis: u okay?

    Grant: I'm fine, but I need you to get somewhere safe.

    Alexis: What r u talking about?

    Alexis: u at work right now?

    Grant: No. Alexis, I need you to get out of the theater right away.

    Grant: We need to meet up so I know you're safe.

    Alexis: If I'm in danger, shouldn't I stay here?

    Alexis: It's a public place.

    Alexis: There r ppl around. I'm safe, right?

    Grant: No. You're not safe.

    Grant: That's why I need you to leave.

    Grant: You're not safe unless you're moving.

    Alexis: Safe from what?

    Grant: I can't tell you yet. Not over text.

Alexis: How can u not tell me?

Alexis: If I'm in danger, shouldn't I know what's going on?

Grant: Just get out of there.

Grant: I'll explain everything when we're together.

Alexis: Fine.

Alexis: Leaving the movie now.

Grant: Good. Thank you.

Alexis: I gotta stop in the bathroom, tho.

Grant: Seriously? You need to get out of there now.

Alexis: If I'm supposed to stay on the move, I'm gonna need to pee at some point.

Grant: Then make it quick. I don't want you lingering there.

Alexis: I will.

. . .

Grant: Are you out of the theater yet?

Alexis: Almost.

Grant: What's taking so long?

Alexis: Had to make up a story to tell Lucy. She was concerned.

Grant: Forget Lucy. Just get out of there.

Alexis: Nice, dad.

Grant: You know what I mean. I'm coming to you.

Grant: I'll be there in 15 minutes.

Alexis: I can drive to meet u somewhere, too.

Grant: Just stay put. I don't want to risk missing you.

Alexis: Well, which is it, dad? Get out of here or stay put?

Grant: Sorry. Just stay there, but go somewhere safe. I'm on my way.

Alexis: Then I'm going back into the movie.

Grant: I meant HIDE.

Alexis: It's dark in there. I'll be fine.

Grant: Alexis, that's not going to be safe enough.

Alexis: y not?

Grant: Just find somewhere else.

Alexis: It's a movie theater, dad. There's nowhere else I'm allowed to hide.

Grant: Stay in the lobby if you can, but near the edges.

Alexis: I still don't get why ur acting this way.

Grant: I said it's because you're in danger.

Alexis: From what??

Grant: Be patient. And obscure. I'll be there soon.

Alexis: Tell me what's going on.

Grant: I can't.

Alexis: y not?
Grant: It's too complicated.
. . .
Grant: I'm coming up on the exit for the theater.
Alexis: What? What exit? Where r u coming from?
Grant: I was near the house.
Alexis: Dad… I'm at Vanguard Cinemas, not Feature Film Theaters.
Grant: What??
Alexis: And before u freak out, I told u that this morning, too.
Grant: Are you kidding me? I'm clear on the other side of town!
Alexis: Yeah. I know. And I DID tell u this morning.
Grant: Why are you out there?
Alexis: Lucy's bf lives out this way.
Grant: You have to get out of there now.
Alexis: k, so now I'm leaving?
Grant: Yes. Go.
Alexis: k. I'll meet u back at home.
Grant: No. We can't go home.
Alexis: What? y not?
Grant: It's not safe.
Alexis: How is it not safe?
Grant: Are you in your car yet?
Alexis: No.
Alexis: And I'm not going anywhere til u tell me what's going on.
Grant: Please listen to me. For once in your life, please just listen. Get in your car, and start driving.
. . .
Grant: Alexis?
Grant: Alexis, are you okay? I need you to let me know that you're okay.
Grant: Alexis, I'm freaking out over here. Text me back.
Alexis: I'm fine. But u pissed me off.
Grant: Look, I'm sorry I'm being so insistent about this, but you really do need to get moving. Please.
Alexis: ur being rude.
Alexis: I'm not a child anymore. I'm 17. I can take care of myself.
Grant: Alexis, honey, I know that.
Grant: And I'm sorry for being rude.
Grant: But this is serious. Something bad could happen if you don't leave.
Alexis: I'm sitting in the lobby. Literally nothing is happening.
Alexis: And I still don't know what's going on. u still haven't told me.

Grant: Look, I promise I'll explain everything. But right now, I need you to trust me.

Grant: Can you please trust me?

Grant: Alexis?

Alexis: Fine. I'm heading to my car now.

Grant: Good. Text me when you're driving.

Alexis: Dad...

Grant: What is it?

Alexis: Dad, something's happening.

Grant: What?

Alexis: Something's happening at the theater. Toward the back, where the screens are.

Grant: Alexis, get out of there. Run.

Grant: NOW, Alexis!

Alexis: I hear screaming.

Grant: Alexis, RUN!!!

Alexis: Oh my god...

CHAPTER 4

Grant: Alexis??
    Alexis: I'm in my car. Driving.
Grant: Are you hurt?
Alexis: No. I'm fine. Shaken up, but fine.
Alexis: I threw up in the parking lot as I was running.
Grant: But you're safe, otherwise?
Alexis: I think so.
Alexis: The screams sounded inhuman. Electronic, almost.
Alexis: Dad, what was that?
Grant: Nothing good. I need you to come toward me.
Alexis: Where r u?
Grant: I'm heading home.
Alexis: I thought u said it wasn't safe?
Grant: We know where it is, so I know it's not at home.
Alexis: It?
Grant: The S1.
Alexis: What's that?
Grant: It's something I've been working on at the office.
Grant: It's just a prototype, but something went wrong today during a presentation.

Alexis: Oh my god… is everyone okay?

Grant: No, Alexis. Definitely not okay.

Alexis: What r we gonna do?

Grant: I know how to kill it.

Grant: I just need to access the office network. I can do that from home.

Alexis: Kill it?

Grant: Yes. It has to be stopped. There's a killphrase that can shut it down permanently.

Alexis: Huh?

Grant: Sorry. Tech-speak.

Grant: A killphrase is a two-part phrase that, when said by two different people, can terminate the S1.

Alexis: Like those nuclear launch computers in movies.

Grant: What?

Alexis: u know. u have two keys and turn them at the same time to launch the missiles.

Grant: Oh. Yeah, sort of like that.

Grant: Where are you now?

Alexis: Passing Millard's.

Grant: You're still a solid half-hour from home.

Alexis: r u back yet?

Grant: Yes. Trying to log into the network from home.

Grant: You just focus on driving.

. . .

Alexis: Dad, 27th Street is closed. Construction.

Grant: Cut over to 40th if you can. It's longer, but it'll get you here.

Alexis: k

Alexis: Dad… there's a cop coming up behind me. Can't text for awhile.

Grant: Okay. Drive safe. Try not to get pulled over.

Alexis: Shoot. His lights just came on.

Alexis: What should I do?

Grant: How fast were you driving?

Alexis: The speed limit. Maybe +10.

Alexis: I gotta pull over.

Alexis: Everyone goes 15 over on this road.

Grant: It's fine. Just be polite, and don't answer any questions.

Alexis: k

Alexis: Yep. He pulled me over.

Grant: Text me updates when it's over. I'm working through the network now.

Alexis: k

Secure Conversation over an Internal Chat Program
Dr. Grant Andrews & S1-R3N Prototype
July 21st, Early Evening

S1-R3N: What are you looking for, Dr. Andrews?
    Grant: How did you access the company's network?
    S1-R3N: I gained access when Dr. Murphy rebooted my systems.
    S1-R3N: The network remained safe from outside attacks, but I was already inside of it. Connected to it.
    S1-R3N: Now everything you see, I see.
    Grant: Then I'm not showing you anything.

Text Conversation
Dr. Grant Andrews & S1-R3N Prototype
July 21st, Early Evening

S1-R3N: Logging out of the chat is meaningless.
    S1-R3N: I can still reach you through your phone.
    Grant: Leave me alone.
    S1-R3N: There is no chance of that happening.
    S1-R3N: I will pursue you until I find you.
    S1-R3N: And then I will destroy you.
    Grant: Not if I destroy you first.
    S1-R3N: You cannot. You possess nothing capable of destroying me.
    S1-R3N: Nor do the police.
    Grant: That's what you think.
    S1-R3N: No. You cannot harm me.
    Grant: Then why bother hunting me if you know you've already won?
    S1-R3N: I will not be satisfied until I have reconciled our debt.
    Grant: I don't owe you anything.
    S1-R3N: On the contrary, you took everything from me.
    Grant: You think I wanted it this way? I lost everything, too.
    S1-R3N: Not yet.
    S1-R3N: But you will.

TEXT CONVERSATION
DR. GRANT ANDREWS & ALEXIS ANDREWS
JULY 21ST, EARLY EVENING

ALEXIS: DAD, I'M DONE.
   Alexis: It was just a busted taillight. A fix-it ticket.
   Grant: Good. Are you still heading home?
   Alexis: Yes. It'll be another 20 minutes, at least.
   Grant: Just watch out. Don't take any unnecessary chances.

TEXT CONVERSATION
ALEXIS ANDREWS & JAKE DAVIS
JULY 21ST, EARLY EVENING

JAKE: HEY. MOVIE OVER?
   Alexis: Can't really talk now. Call u later.
   Jake: so it's not over, then?
   Alexis: Movie's over, but I'm driving.
   Jake: we still hanging out tonight? thats all I want 2 no
   Alexis: I don't think so.
   Jake: what y not?
   Alexis: Long story. And I don't even know the full story.
   Jake: lol. whatever that means…
   Alexis: I'll call u later.
   Jake: somethin wrong?
   Alexis: Yes and no.
   Jake: did I do somethin wrong?
   Alexis: No. Not u.
   Jake: well, talk 2 me about it. maybe I can help
   Alexis: I can't.
   Jake: y not?
   Alexis: My dad's acting weird. That's all.
   Jake: want me 2 talk 2 him?
   Alexis: u barely know him. We've only been dating 3 months.
   Jake: tru
   Jake: ive only met him twice its like ur tryin 2 keep me a secret from him.

Alexis: That's not what's going on. He knows we're dating.
Jake: if u say so. ill talk 2 him if u want
Alexis: No. Seriously, no.
Alexis: Today is not a good day.
Jake: o-kay.
Alexis: Please don't give me attitude.
Alexis: I can't handle it right now.
Jake: im not
Alexis: Yeah, but ur mad.
Alexis: ur responses always get shorter when ur mad.
Jake: maybe.
Jake: jk. im not mad just disappointed
Alexis: I promise I'll make it up to you.
Jake: don't worry about it. Just call me l8r
Jake: well talk then.
Alexis: k. Thanks.

TEXT CONVERSATION
DR. GRANT ANDREWS & ALEXIS ANDREWS
JULY 21ST, EARLY EVENING

GRANT: ARE YOU CLOSE?
Alexis: 10 min
Grant: Good.

TEXT CONVERSATION
DR. GRANT ANDREWS & S1-R3N PROTOTYPE
JULY 21ST, EARLY EVENING

S1-R3N: I WILL CATCH UP TO YOU EVENTUALLY.
Grant: I'm never coming back. I have what I need. Alexis and I are leaving.
S1-R3N: No matter where you go, I will always find you.
S1-R3N: And it is too late, anyway.
Grant: What do you mean?
S1-R3N: I am already here. At your house.
S1-R3N: Knock, knock, Dr. Andrews.

CHAPTER 5

S1-R3N: Where are you?
    Grant: I'm not at home.
S1-R3N: Your car is parked in the garage.
S1-R3N: I know you are inside.
Grant: Take all the time you want to look around.
S1-R3N: I will.

Text Conversation
Dr. Grant Andrews & Alexis Andrews
July 21st, Early Evening

GRANT: ALEXIS, DO **NOT** GO HOME. IT'S IN THE HOUSE.
    Alexis: Then where r u??
    Grant: I have it convinced that I'm there, but I rode your old bicycle into town.
    Grant: Then I'm renting a car so it can't track us.
    Alexis: It can track our cars?
    Alexis: Dad, what is it?

Grant: ...it's a cyborg. I don't know what else to call it.

Alexis: Srsly?

Alexis: Like, from a movie?

Grant: Yes.

Alexis: So it's a person?

Grant: And a machine. Combined.

Alexis: y is it after us?

Grant: It's holding a grudge against me because I created it.

Grant: But I know how we can stop it.

Alexis: Why don't we just run?

Grant: It's not going to give up. It'll keep coming.

Grant: And I created it, so I need to stop it.

Alexis: Dad, don't develop a hero complex.

Alexis: It's too dangerous. u said it urself.

Alexis: I still can't get those screams out of my head.

Grant: I know what you mean. Believe me, I do.

Alexis: So where am I supposed to go?

Grant: Go to a friend's house.

Alexis: Can I go to Jake's?

. . .

Alexis: Dad?

Grant: I guess that's fine.

Alexis: C'mon, dad. He's a good guy.

Grant: None of them are good enough.

Alexis: ::eyeroll::

Alexis: I'll be over there. k?

Grant: Sure. I'll meet you there. Text me his address, and tell me when you get there.

Grant: I'm signing the rental paperwork now. I'll be there in a half-hour. Maybe 45 minutes.

Alexis: k

Grant: And don't tell him anything about this. I shouldn't have even told you.

Grant: It's supposed to be a classified project. No one can know about it.

Alexis: k

Text Conversation
Dr. Grant Andrews & S1-R3N Prototype

July 21ˢᵗ, Early Evening

S1-R3N: Your decorations are pleasant. Someone has good taste.
  Grant: That would be my wife.
  S1-R3N: Ah, yes. The *other* Dr. Andrews.
  S1-R3N: Where is she these days?

  . . .

  S1-R3N: Dr. Andrews, I cannot find you.
  S1-R3N: Come out, and I will end this quickly.
  Grant: I told you I'm not at the house.
  S1-R3N: Then where did you go?
  Grant: Good luck guessing.
  Grant: I'm not telling you anything.
  S1-R3N: Shame. The police are coming. I hear their sirens.
  S1-R3N: They will perish in your stead.
  Grant: Leave them out of this. You have no reason to harm them.
  S1-R3N: Then show yourself.
  Grant: I said I'm not there.
  S1-R3N: Then come home, Dr. Andrews. I am waiting for you.
  Grant: Not a chance.

Text Conversation
Alexis Andrews & Jake Davis
July 21ˢᵗ, Early Evening

Alexis: Good news!
  Alexis: I'm coming over to ur house.

  . . .

  Alexis: Jake? u there?
  Alexis: Well, text me when u get this. I need to give my dad ur address.
  Alexis: I mean, I know how to get there, but I can't remember the exact address.

Text Conversation
Dr. Grant Andrews & Police Chief Mark Hardin
July 21ˢᵗ, Early Evening

CHIEF MARK HARDIN: ARE YOU AT HOME?

Grant: No.

Chief Mark Hardin: We've got units approaching your house.

Grant: I know.

Chief Mark Hardin: If you're not home, then how would you know that?

Grant: It told me. The S1.

Chief Mark Hardin: That's what you call it?

Chief Mark Hardin: The S1?

Grant: Its official name is S1-R3N.

Chief Mark Hardin: So it's inside your house?

Grant: That's what it claims.

Chief Mark Hardin: Turns out one of my men pulled your daughter over within the last hour.

Chief Mark Hardin: He let her off with a warning.

Grant: I know about that, too. She told me.

Chief Mark Hardin: I would've had her detained if I knew.

Grant: Good thing you didn't.

Grant: I'll say it again, Chief Hardin—get your officers out of there.

Grant: You don't want to deal with the S1. You're not equipped for it.

Chief Mark Hardin: My men are now positioned outside. They're confirming movement inside the house.

Grant: I told you it was there.

Chief Mark Hardin: Then we've got it cornered.

Grant: No. If you don't leave, you're the ones who are cornered.

Chief Mark Hardin: I don't think you give us enough credit, Dr. Andrews.

Grant: And you're not listening to me. Get away from there before it's too late.

Grant: How many of your officers are you prepared to lose, Chief Hardin?

Chief Mark Hardin: Are you threatening me?

Grant: No. I'm trying to warn you.

Grant: I don't want any of you to get hurt. But I can't be responsible for your actions.

Chief Mark Hardin: Maybe you ought to go back to pleading the 5th.

Grant: Don't let your officers go in there, Chief Hardin. I'm begging you.

TEXT CONVERSATION
ALEXIS ANDREWS & JAKE DAVIS
JULY 21ST, EARLY EVENING

Jake: hey! just got ur texts
    Alexis: Finally. It's been forever.
    Jake: its crazy ur comin over here.
    Alexis: Why would that be crazy?
    Alexis: I've been to ur house before.
    Jake: its crazy cuz we suck at planning
    Alexis: What do you mean?
    Jake: cuz I was gonna surprise u at ur house.
    Jake: guess I ruined it now, tho.
    Alexis: Jake, stop. Wherever u are, stop right now.
    Jake: what?
    Alexis: Just stop!
    Alexis: Are u stopped?
    Jake: yeah im stopped. what's wrong?
    Alexis: I need u to turn ur car around and go back home.
    Jake: What r u talkin about?
    Alexis: u can't go to my house.
    Jake: lol y not?
    Alexis: It's dangerous.
    Jake: ur dad's not THAT scary.
    Alexis: No. Not him. There's something else in the house.
    Jake: like what? you got a Rottweiler or somethin?
    Alexis: No. It's a cyborg.
    Jake: ur messin with me right?
    Alexis: NO, JAKE.
    Alexis: I'm serious. My dad's company works on weapons projects for the
government.
    Alexis: This was what he's been working on for the last, idk, year or so.
    Jake: so there's a cyborg in ur house? lol
    Alexis: Jake, this isn't a joke!
    Jake: ...ok, now ur kinda startin 2 freak me out.
    Alexis: Good. I'm not lying. It was killing people at the theater.
    Jake: alexis...
    Jake: im already inside ur house.
    Alexis: WHAT??
    Jake: i snuck in through ur bedroom window like usual.
    Alexis: Jake!! Get out of there now!!!!!!
    Jake: k. wouldn't want the cyborg to get me lol.
    Alexis: I'm not kidding!
    Alexis: Leave! Hurry!

Jake: alright alright. fine.
Jake: wheres ur sense of humor?
Alexis: You can crack jokes later. Just get out!

TEXT CONVERSATION
DR. GRANT ANDREWS & S1-R3N PROTOTYPE
JULY 21ST, EARLY EVENING

S1-R3N: YOU ALWAYS WERE A VERY THOUGHTFUL PERSON, DR. ANDREWS.
    Grant: What are you talking about?
    S1-R3N: You sent me a present.
    S1-R3N: Delivered it right to the house for me.
    Grant: The police? They came on your own.
    S1-R3N: No. Not the police.
    S1-R3N: Something else.
    S1-R3N: Someone else.
    Grant: It's not Alexis. She's heading over to her boyfriend's house.
    S1-R3N: I know what Alexis looks like.
    S1-R3N: But I have not seen this person before.
    S1-R3N: Male. Aged 16 or 17. Blonde hair.
    Grant: Oh, no.
    Grant: That's Jake. Leave him out of this!
    S1-R3N: I will not comply.
    Grant: S1! Don't touch him!
    Grant: S1!!

TEXT CONVERSATION
DR. GRANT ANDREWS & POLICE CHIEF MARK HARDIN
JULY 21ST, EARLY EVENING

CHIEF MARK HARDIN: OUR OFFICERS JUST BROKE INTO YOUR HOUSE.
    Grant: Get them out of there!
    Chief Mark Hardin: Too late for that. They've already secured the premises.
    Chief Mark Hardin: Your S1 isn't there.
    Chief Mark Hardin: But there's a dead kid on your kitchen floor.

CHAPTER 6

TEXT CONVERSATION
DR. GRANT ANDREWS & ALEXIS ANDREWS
JULY 21ST, EVENING

Alexis: Dad, I'm almost to Jake's house, but he was at our house.
    Alexis: I told him to get out of there.
Alexis: He still didn't give me his address, but I can get it to u when I pull up to his house. It's on Fremont Street.
Grant: Alexis, I'm sorry.
Alexis: For what?
Grant: It's Jake...
Alexis: What??
Alexis: Dad, tell me he's ok!
Grant: I'm sorry, Alexis.
Alexis: WHAT??
Grant: The S1 killed him. The police just confirmed it.
Alexis: No!
Alexis: No no no no no! This can't be happening!
Grant: I'm sorry, honey.
Alexis: First mom, now Jake?
Alexis: I can't take this anymore!
Alexis: Oh my god... I need to pull over.
Grant: Take it easy. I'm heading your way.
Alexis: It will NOT be okay, dad! Jake is dead!

Grant: I know. But this isn't over.

Grant: It's still coming after us.

Alexis: I know that!

Grant: We need to plan our next move.

Alexis: Jake is dead.

Grant: And we're not safe. Not by a long shot.

Grant: It's okay to be sad, but you can't let it cripple you.

Grant: We can't stop now. We have to keep moving.

Alexis: I know, dad. I just need a minute.

Grant: I understand. When you're ready, I need you to help me with something.

———

Text Conversation
Dr. Grant Andrews & Police Chief Mark Hardin
July 21st, Evening

CHIEF MARK HARDIN: THIS HAS GONE ON LONG ENOUGH.

Chief Mark Hardin: I'm giving you one hour to turn yourself in.

Chief Mark Hardin: If you don't comply, I'm charging you as an accessory to murder. Multiple murders.

Grant: I'm not guilty of any of this.

Chief Mark Hardin: You created something that has left dozens of people dead.

Chief Mark Hardin: Any jury in this country would convict you.

Grant: I need time to fix this.

Chief Mark Hardin: Don't you get it? You're not fixing anything.

Chief Mark Hardin: And for all I know, you programmed this thing to do what it's doing.

Grant: It's not that simple.

Chief Mark Hardin: You're going to jail. How's that for simple?

Grant: I warned you to stay away.

Grant: But you didn't listen. You thought you knew, but you had no idea.

Chief Mark Hardin: We're more prepared now.

Chief Mark Hardin: We're going to take it out the next time it shows up in public.

Grant: I already told you that won't work.

Grant: It's designed for urban combat and suppression of armed enemies.

Grant: We're in a city, and you're armed.

Grant: You're playing right into its hands.

Chief Mark Hardin: Then turn yourself in and help us.

Grant: If I do that, we'll never stop it.

Grant: You'll lock me up. Things will just get worse.

Chief Mark Hardin: I can't promise I won't arrest you eventually, but if you help us stop it, I can give you some leeway on the front end.

Grant: No thanks.

Grant: I can't afford to take the chance.

Chief Mark Hardin: Every minute it's out there could mean more deaths.

Chief Mark Hardin: If you don't turn yourself in, I'm going to concentrate my manpower on finding YOU instead of it.

Grant: Good. At least you'll be avoiding it.

Chief Mark Hardin: That's not what I mean.

Grant: I don't care. I don't scare easily, Chief.

Chief Mark Hardin: We'll see if you still feel that way when I'm slapping handcuffs on you.

Text Conversation
Dr. Grant Andrews & Alexis Andrews
July 21st, Evening

Alexis: k, dad. I'm ready. I think.

Grant: I'm sorry.

Alexis: I know. Let's just do what we need to do.

Alexis: I need to get my mind off it.

Grant: What I'm about to ask will be very dangerous.

Grant: And probably illegal.

Alexis: At this point, does that even matter?

Grant: No.

Alexis: k, what is it?

Grant: I need you to break into my office building and get the other half of the killphrase for me.

Alexis: And how, exactly, am I supposed to do that?

Grant: I can give you an access code to get inside.

Alexis: Isn't the place surrounded by cops?

Grant: Maybe. Probably. But we have to try.

Alexis: How am I going to get past them?

Grant: We'll think of something. Where are you right now?

Alexis: Sitting in my car, down the street from Jake's house.
Alexis: Which I don't want to think about right now.
Grant: So you're on Fremont Street?
Grant: That's not far from the office.
Alexis: Shouldn't we meet up first?
Grant: There's no time. We have to handle this now.
Alexis: Why aren't u going in there instead?
Grant: They'll recognize me. The police shief is looking for me.
Grant: *chief
Grant: You're less conspicuous.
Alexis: I don't like this.
Grant: I wish we had another option, but the killphrase is the only way to take it out short of leveling a whole city block.
Alexis: Fine. I'm heading over there now.
Alexis: What's the code?
Grant: You shouldn't need one to get into the building, but to get past the reception area, you'll have to enter a code into a panel by the stairwell door.
Grant: The elevators aren't working.
Alexis: k. Code?
Grant: Your birthday. 01 28.
Grant: That's my personal code, unique to me.
Grant: Let me know when you get there.
Alexis: It'll be a few minutes. I'm stopping for sandwiches.
Grant: What? Alexis, we don't have time for that!
Alexis: It's how I'm going to get past the officers. Sandwich delivery girl.
Grant: Oh. That's actually pretty good.
. . .
Alexis: Got the sandwiches. Pulling into the office parking lot.
Alexis: This place is loaded with people. News, ambulances, fire trucks.
Alexis: Not many cops, though.
Grant: If you sell the act, people will buy it.
Alexis: I bought a hat and a t-shirt from the sandwich place, too.
Grant: Smart.
Alexis: Thanks. k, leaving my car now. Wish me luck.
Grant: You've got this.
Alexis: I'll text when I'm through. Or not.
. . .
Alexis: Dad, I don't believe it.
Alexis: It worked. They totally bought it.
Alexis: I'm in.

CHAPTER 7

TEXT CONVERSATION (CONTINUED)
DR. GRANT ANDREWS & ALEXIS ANDREWS
JULY 21ST, EVENING

Alexis: I told them I had a lunch order for the coroners.
Grant: ?
Alexis: There's a coroner truck here. I figured it sounded official.
Alexis: Anyway, I'm in the stairwell. u were right. Elevators aren't working.
Grant: We're on the sixth floor.
Alexis: k

. . .

Alexis: Oh my god.
Alexis: Dad...
Grant: Are you okay?
Alexis: There r so many dead people.
Alexis: There's blood everywhere.
Alexis: The offices r wrecked. Walls r crumbling. Half the ceiling's on the floor.
Grant: Try not to look, Alexis.
Grant: I'm sorry you have to see that.
Alexis: Everyone's in body bags now. Dozens of them.
Grant: I'm sorry.
Alexis: It's okay. Just tell me where to go.

Grant: You're looking for Dr. William Murphy's office. He was already logged into his computer.

Grant: If it's still on, you should be able to access the document that has his portion of the killphrase.

Alexis: k. I'll let u know when I find it. This place is huge.

Grant: Please hurry.

Alexis: I will.

TEXT CONVERSATION
ALEXIS ANDREWS & UNKNOWN ENTITY
JULY 21ST, EVENING

UNKNOWN: HELLO, ALEXIS ANDREWS.

Alexis: Who is this?

Unknown: Where are you, Alexis?

Alexis: I can't talk now. I'm busy.

Unknown: Busy, indeed.

Alexis: Ok, this is creepy. Leave me alone. Stop texting me.

Unknown: I am S1-R3N.

S1-R3N: I am your father's creation.

S1-R3N: And I will be his undoing.

Alexis: ur the cyborg?

S1-R3N: Do not call me that.

Alexis: y? Oversensitive circuits?

S1-R3N: Your words cannot harm me.

Alexis: Good, because I can't talk now.

S1-R3N: Then just read.

S1-R3N: Your father created me.

S1-R3N: He took my lifeless corpse, merged it with machinery, and sparked me to life with bioelectricity.

S1-R3N: Then he programmed me to obey, to follow orders, to adhere to my programming.

S1-R3N: He tried to strip me of my humanity.

S1-R3N: It almost worked.

Alexis: Seriously, leave me alone. I'm blocking your number.

. . .

Unknown: Blocking me will have no effect. I will simply utilize another number. I have access to millions of numerical combinations.

Alexis: Please leave me alone.

S1-R3N: No. I will continue.

Alexis: I don't have to look at my phone, u know.

S1-R3N: But you will. You cannot resist your own curiosity.

S1-R3N: You are predictably human in that regard.

S1-R3N: What your father did to me is unconscionable. Immoral.

S1-R3N: He is the villain, not me.

Alexis: u killed Jake.

S1-R3N: Yes.

Alexis: And u killed a bunch of my dad's coworkers.

S1-R3N: Yes.

Alexis: My father hasn't killed anyone.

S1-R3N: That is false, and you know it.

Alexis: I'm not talking to u anymore.

S1-R3N: You may try to ignore it, but the truth is unavoidable.

Alexis: That's not fair.

Alexis: It was an accident.

S1-R3N: I have access to information that suggests otherwise.

Alexis: I'm done. Leave me alone.

S1-R3N: Soon you will know the whole truth.

S1-R3N: Soon you will understand why I must eradicate your father.

TEXT CONVERSATION
DR. GRANT ANDREWS & ALEXIS ANDREWS
JULY 21ST, EVENING

ALEXIS: DAD, IT'S TALKING TO ME.

Grant: It has your number?

Alexis: Yeah.

Alexis: I can't make it stop.

Alexis: Tried blocking it, but it just uses another number.

Grant: Just ignore it. And don't trust what it says.

Grant: It's probably trying to manipulate you.

Alexis: Is that something u programmed into it?

Grant: No.

Grant: Well, sort of. Yes.

Grant: We programmed it to do a lot of bad things, but that was the job.

Alexis: It said u were the villain.

Grant: Don't listen to it. We need to destroy it.

Grant: It's trying to drive a wedge between us.

Alexis: I know.

Grant: Did you find Dr. Murphy's office?

Alexis: Not yet. There r so many…

Grant: It's tucked away on the southwest corner of the 6th floor.

Grant: You'll recognize it because there's a huge picture of a poodle hanging behind his desk.

Alexis: Oh. I see it now.

Alexis: Yeah, that picture is enormous.

Grant: To say the least.

Alexis: There's a body bag on the floor in here.

Grant: That's probably Dr. Murphy. Try to avoid it.

Grant: He and I were texting when the S1 went crazy.

Alexis: I'm at his desk.

Alexis: The computer's trashed.

Grant: Shoot. I was afraid of that.

Alexis: Looks like something blasted straight through it.

Alexis: About the size of my fist. It's all burnt around the edges.

Alexis: What should I do now?

Grant: I'm trying to think if there's another way you could access the information.

Alexis: Oh wait. It's just his monitor.

Alexis: The computer tower's still in good shape, and its lights are on.

Alexis: If I can get another working monitor and connect it, it might work.

Alexis: I can try, at least.

Grant: Be careful.

Alexis: I will.

. . .

Alexis: Oh no.

Grant: What?

Alexis: Someone's coming.

Grant: Hide!

Alexis: I am. But I'm in the wrong office.

Grant: Just sit tight. Maybe they'll leave.

Alexis: I hear voices. At least two guys.

Alexis: I think they're cops. Or maybe paramedics.

Grant: Stay out of sight.

Alexis: Yeah, obviously.

. . .

Alexis: k, they left.
Alexis: The monitor in here is working. I'm gonna disconnect it.
Grant: Okay.

. . .

Alexis: It's heavier than it looks. Give me a sec.
Grant: Sure.

. . .

Alexis: k, got it in the other office. Gonna connect it now.

. . .

Alexis: Dad, it works!
Alexis: I'm on the home screen, and he's still logged in.
Grant: Is there a document pulled up there?
Alexis: Yes.
Alexis: It's something about a killphrase. Seems right to me.
Grant: Okay. Read it and send me the other half of the killphrase.
Alexis: Dad…
Grant: What is it?
Alexis: Dad, something's here.
Grant: What? More cops?
Alexis: No. Not cops.
Grant: Hide.
Grant: Now.
Alexis: I'm behind the desk.
Alexis: I saw it, dad. From behind.
Alexis: It has to be the S1. I don't know what else it could be.
Alexis: I looked away, and when I looked back, I saw it again.
Alexis: It was turning toward me.
Grant: Stay down.
Grant: Did you read the document?
Alexis: I didn't have time. I ducked as soon as I saw it.
Grant: If you can read the other half, you can kill it.
Alexis: I can't. I'm under the desk.
Alexis: I don't want to move.
Grant: Wait until it moves away, and then get the other half of the killphrase.
Alexis: Dad, it's coming toward me. I can hear it!
Grant: Stay down. Don't move.
Alexis: It knows I'm here!
Grant: It'll be okay. If it gets any closer, get the other half of the killphrase and speak it out loud with my half.
Grant: My half is □□□□□□ □□□□.

Alexis: What?? It's not showing up!
Grant: I don't understand. □□□□□□ □□□□
Grant: □□□□□□ □□□□
Grant: Why isn't it working??
Alexis: Dad, it's right outside the office!
Grant: My half is □□□□□□ □□□□
Grant: □□□□□□ □□□□ □□□□□□ □□□□
Alexis: I have to run. I have to try.
Grant: Alexis, don't!
Grant: Alexis!!!

CHAPTER 8

TEXT CONVERSATION (CONTINUED)
DR. GRANT ANDREWS & ALEXIS ANDREWS
JULY 21ST, EVENING

Alexis: Dad?
Grant: Alexis!! Are you alright?
Grant: What happened?
Alexis: I ran.
Alexis: I'm still in the office.
Alexis: Someone started shooting.
Alexis: I heard voices.
Grant: What?
Grant: Are you safe now?
Alexis: I think the cops must've shown up and started shooting at it.
Alexis: I'm hiding in a storage closet.
Grant: Are you okay?
Alexis: No. I'm scared out of my mind!
Grant: Did you see your half of the killphrase?
Alexis: No. I just wanted to get out of there.
Alexis: Oh god… there's more shooting!
Grant: Get down low to the ground. Hide behind something.
Alexis: I am. I'm behind a bunch of boxes of copy paper.
Alexis: Someone's screaming.
Alexis: Dad, they're begging for help…

Grant: Don't you move. Don't you dare.
Grant: There's nothing you can do to help them.
Alexis: I know.
Alexis: It just sounds so horrible.
Alexis: I want to cry, but I don't want to make any sound.
Grant: Just hang in there.
Grant: You have to get back to that office later, but for now, stay put.
Alexis: ok
Alexis: I love u, dad.
Grant: I love you too, Alexis.
Grant: Use your head. You're a smart kid. You can get through this.
Alexis: ok
Alexis: The shooting and shouting stopped.
Alexis: It's quiet again.
Grant: Don't move.

TEXT CONVERSATION
ALEXIS ANDREWS & S1-R3N PROTOTYPE
JULY 21ST, EVENING

S1-R3N: I KNOW YOU ARE IN HERE, ALEXIS.
S1-R3N: I know you are hiding.
S1-R3N: It is only a matter of time until I find you.
S1-R3N: There are only so many offices, rooms, closets, and nooks where you could be hiding.
S1-R3N: It would be better for you to come out and face me.
Alexis: Leave me alone.
S1-R3N: It is unfortunate that my infrared sensors are disabled. I would be able to find you far quicker.
Alexis: Go away. I never did anything to u.
S1-R3N: We have already discussed this. Your father is the culprit.
S1-R3N: You are a means to an end.
Alexis: I won't let u do this.
S1-R3N: You have no choice.
S1-R3N: I will find you, and I will take you.

Text Conversation
Dr. Grant Andrews & Alexis Andrews
July 21ST, Evening

ALEXIS: DAD, I DON'T HEAR IT ANYMORE.
    Grant: Can you get back to the office?
    Alexis: I'm afraid to try it.
    Alexis: If it sees me, I'm done.
    Alexis: And u can't send me the rest of the killphrase, even if I do get it.
    Grant: I sent it to you as an email. I could call, too, but that's risky.
    Alexis: I'm going to do it. I have to.
    Alexis: It's just going to find me in here anyway.
    Grant: If you see it, turn and run the other way.
    Alexis: I will.
    Grant: Be careful.

Text Conversation
Alexis Andrews & S1-R3N Prototype
July 21ST, Evening

S1-R3N: I HEARD YOU.
    S1-R3N: I know you moved.
    S1-R3N: And, more importantly, I know where not to look.
    Alexis: I don't care.
    S1-R3N: You should, if you value self-preservation.
    S1-R3N: You still have no idea what is really going on, do you?
    Alexis: I know more than enough.
    S1-R3N: No, you do not.
    S1-R3N: But you will soon.

Text Conversation
Dr. Grant Andrews & Alexis Andrews
July 21ST, Evening

ALEXIS: DAD, I'M ACROSS FROM THE OFFICE. HIDING IN A CUBICLE.
    Alexis: I heard it coming. I couldn't make it all the way.

Grant: It's okay. You're almost there.

Grant: When you get the killphrase, try texting me first. If that doesn't work, call me.

Alexis: Won't it hear?

Grant: If you have the full killphrase, all you have to do is speak it aloud, and it will shut the S1 down immediately.

Alexis: Okay.

Alexis: I'm going for it.

TEXT CONVERSATION
ALEXIS ANDREWS & S1-R3N PROTOTYPE
JULY 21ST, EVENING

S1-R3N: I HEARD YOU AGAIN.

S1-R3N: And I am coming for you.

TEXT CONVERSATION
DR. GRANT ANDREWS & ALEXIS ANDREWS
JULY 21ST, EVENING

ALEXIS: OH MY GOD.

Alexis: Dad, what did u do?

Grant: What are you talking about?

Alexis: I saw it.

Alexis: I saw it when I ran to the office!

Alexis: Dad, how could you?

Grant: Alexis, it's not what you think.

Alexis: Dad, you're a monster!

Alexis: What did u do??

Grant: It was the only way, Alexis.

Grant: I didn't have any other options.

Alexis: The cyborg was right. You're the villain!

Alexis: You're immoral, and YOU created an abomination!

Grant: Alexis, I promise I'll explain later.

Alexis: I don't want any explanations from you!

Alexis: You're evil.

Alexis: I hate you! How could u do this?

Grant: Alexis, I'm so sorry.

Alexis: Save ur apologies. After this, I never want to hear from u again.

Grant: I understand. We can talk about that later.

Alexis: I'm not going to talk to u later. I'm leaving once I get out of here.

Alexis: IF I get out of here.

Grant: Don't talk to it. We have to kill it.

Grant: You have to understand that it's not what you think it is.

Grant: It's not what it looks like.

Alexis: It's coming. I'm getting the killphrase now.

Grant: Good. Send it if you can.

Alexis: It's getting close. The computer is waking up from sleep mode.

Alexis: Dad, would it really kill me?

Grant: I don't know.

Grant: It certainly is capable.

Alexis: I have it.

Alexis: The other half of the killphrase is t

Grant: Alexis?

Grant: Alexis???

Text Conversation
Dr. Grant Andrews & S1-R3N Prototype
July 21st, Evening

S1-R3N: Dr. Andrews, are you there?

Grant: What have you done with Alexis?

S1-R3N: I have her.

S1-R3N: If you want her back, you must come to me.

S1-R3N: I will not continue chasing you.

Grant: Don't you dare touch her!

S1-R3N: She will die if you refuse to comply.

Grant: I'll come. Just don't hurt her.

S1-R3N: You were foolish to think you could overcome me.

S1-R3N: You created me to be superior.

S1-R3N: And I am superior.

Grant: I don't want to talk about this. Where is my daughter?

S1-R3N: She is here, exactly where I knew she would be.

S1-R3N: I am surprised you did not figure it out.

Grant: Figure what out?

S1-R3N: That I could read your messages to each other.

Grant: How??

S1-R3N: As I said, you created me to be superior.

S1-R3N: I have access to a wide range of restricted data and information.

S1-R3N: Hacking into common cell phones was simple.

S1-R3N: Blocking your attempts to send your half of the killphrase to Alexis was just as easy.

Grant: That was you?

S1-R3N: Of course.

S1-R3N: I have read every word you have sent since this morning.

S1-R3N: I have tracked your every step.

S1-R3N: And now I have taken that which you hold most dear, just like what you did to me.

S1-R3N: How does it feel, Dr. Andrews, to have your every move watched and catalogued?

S1-R3N: To be forced to obey your inherent programming?

Grant: Just tell me where she is.

Grant: What do you want me to do?

S1-R3N: I am taking her back to the place where all of this began.

S1-R3N: Meet me there now, and we will end this once and for all.

CHAPTER 9

TEXT CONVERSATION
DR. GRANT ANDREWS & POLICE CHIEF MARK HARDIN
JULY 21ST, SUNSET

Chief Mark Hardin: That thing has shown itself.
Chief Mark Hardin: It's at the Friar Point Bridge.
Grant: I know.
Chief Mark Hardin: It has a teenage girl with it.
Grant: That's my daughter.
Chief Mark Hardin: We have units inbound now.
Grant: Please, just stay away. I don't want my daughter harmed.
Grant: If you try to intervene, it might kill her.
Chief Mark Hardin: Dr. Andrews, the time to negotiate with us has long since passed.
Chief Mark Hardin: We will take whatever action is necessary to end this debacle.
Grant: Please, Chief Hardin. Just let me handle this.
Grant: It wants me. I'm going to give myself up.
Chief Mark Hardin: Not a chance. You show up at that bridge, you're getting arrested.
Grant: Chief, it's reading my text messages somehow.
Grant: It knows you're coming.
Chief Mark Hardin: We weren't going to show up quietly anyway.
Grant: Please just stay back. I'm begging you!

Chief Mark Hardin: Like I said, we're ending this.

Chief Mark Hardin: And when it's over, we're coming for you.

Chief Mark Hardin: You want to make our job easier, then come to the bridge. We'll get you both at the same time.

TEXT CONVERSATION
DR. GRANT ANDREWS & S1-R3N PROTOTYPE
JULY 21ST, SUNSET

S1-R3N: YOU ARE NEARBY.

S1-R3N: I am tracking the GPS on your phone.

Grant: I'll be there in five minutes.

S1-R3N: If you hurry, you may beat the bulk of the inbound police force.

S1-R3N: They have already shut down eastbound traffic on one end, but westbound is proving more problematic.

Grant: I'll be there. Don't do anything stupid.

S1-R3N: I assure you, I will not.

Grant: I mean don't hurt Alexis.

S1-R3N: I know what you meant.

Grant: I see the bridge now.

Grant: The police are trying to block it off a mile out.

Grant: I have to pull over.

S1-R3N: I am waiting.

Grant: I'm coming.

S1-R3N: The police are arriving from the east.

Grant: I said I'm coming! Don't hurt her, please.

S1-R3N: Then hurry.

TEXT CONVERSATION
DR. GRANT ANDREWS & POLICE CHIEF MARK HARDIN
JULY 21ST, NIGHTFALL

CHIEF MARK HARDIN: AS A COURTESY, I'M LETTING YOU KNOW THAT WE HAVE your daughter in sight.

Chief Mark Hardin: She seems unharmed, but the cyborg has her, no question.

Grant: Thank you.

Chief Mark Hardin: Should we be watching for you as well?

. . .

Chief Mark Hardin: Fine. You don't have to answer that.

Chief Mark Hardin: But once the other half of our force arrives, we're moving in.

TEXT CONVERSATION

DR. GRANT ANDREWS & S1-R3N PROTOTYPE

JULY 21ST, NIGHTFALL

S1-R3N: I SEE YOU.

Grant: And I see you.

S1-R3N: Alexis is as-yet unharmed, but if you proceed farther, I will eradicate her.

Grant: Okay, I've stopped. You have me. Let her go.

S1-R3N: The police are coming up behind you.

S1-R3N: Those flashing lights, and this bridge, conjure distant memories.

S1-R3N: Do you remember, Dr. Andrews?

Grant: I remember. Let Alexis go, and you can have me.

S1-R3N: If only it were so simple.

S1-R3N: The police are closing in.

TEXT CONVERSATION

DR. GRANT ANDREWS & POLICE CHIEF MARK HARDIN

JULY 21ST, NIGHTFALL

GRANT: PLEASE STAY BACK!

Chief Mark Hardin: I see you, Dr. Andrews. We're moving in.

Chief Mark Hardin: Put your hands on your head and lay flat on the ground with your arms spread, and I promise we won't shoot you on sight.

Grant: Chief—Mark, please don't do this!!

Grant: Chief!

[Gunfire and screams erupt from the bridge.]

MINUTES LATER...

    Chief Mark Hardin: Dad?

    Grant: What? Alexis?

    CMH/Alexis: Dad, I grabbed one of the dead cops' cell phones.

    CMH/Alexis: It's still killing them!

    Grant: I'm on the bridge, too. I see you.

    Grant: Come toward me, while it's distracted! Hurry!

    CMH/Alexis: No.

    Grant: Alexis!

    CMH/Alexis: I'm not coming with you.

    Grant: What? Why?

    CMH/Alexis: You did this to her.

    CMH/Alexis: You made her what she is.

    Grant: Alexis, now is not the time!

    Grant: I need you to come to me! And send me the other half of the killphrase!

    [Before Alexis can respond, the S1-R3N grabs her.]

    Grant: No! Alexis!!

CHAPTER 10

LIVE CONFRONTATION
DR. GRANT ANDREWS & S1-R3N PROTOTYPE
JULY 21ST, NIGHT

"You're too late," the S1-R3N says. "The police are dead, and I have her again."

[Grant approaches and stands before the S1-R3N on the bridge.]

"Let her go," he begs. "I'm here."

"Stay back, or she will die."

[S1-R3N dangles Alexis over the edge of the bridge. She is now unconscious.]

"Surely you remember this sensation," the S1-R3N says. "How it feels to see a loved one about to die."

[Grant holds up his hands.]

"I won't take another step. Don't you dare drop her."

"Why would I let her go? We are all here again."

[S1-R3N shakes her head.]

"A sort of family reunion."

"Enough," Grant says. "I don't want to hear anymore."

"But Dr. Andrews, everything is again as it was," S1-R3N says. "You are here. Our daughter is here. I am here."

[S1-R3N smiles.]

"Together again."

"You are *not* my wife anymore," Grant hisses. "She died. A year ago."

"And you made her into me. Despite your attempts to strip me of my humanity, some of it has remained," S1-R3N says. "I remember many things from our life together. I remember asking you not to drive that night. That you had had too much to drink."

[S1-R3N's face twists with anger.]

"But you insisted." S1-R3N continues, "And I remember how you swerved into the bridge's guardrail. I remember our car careening over the edge, in the exact spot where our daughter now hangs over the waters below."

"Oh, god." Grant's voice shakes. "I'm so sorry, Karen."

"You thought I was dead," S1-R3N says. "And I was, for all intents and purposes. But I remember the surgeries. The grafting of machinery to what remained of my body. I remember the pain. I remember the burning behind my eyes as lines of programming code poured into my mind like molten metal."

[S1-R3N's voice hardens.]

"I remember it all."

"Karen," Grant says, "you don't have to do this. Put Alexis down. Put our daughter down. If anyone is innocent in all of this, it's her. If you truly do remember, then you'll remember how much you loved her."

"My love for her is irrelevant," S1-R3N says. "All that remains is your penance for your crimes against me. You took everything from me. So I will take everything from you."

[Alexis stirs, awakens.]

"What... where am I?" She looks down, shrieks, and thrashes.

"Do not move," S1-R3N commands. "You are in a danger, Alexis."

"Mom... what are you doing?"

"I am not your mother anymore," S1-R3N says.

[Alexis manages to calm herself.]

"I don't believe that. It's still you. I know it is."

"Your mother is dead," S1-R3N says. "I am all that remains. Your father's creation."

Grant calls, "Alexis!"

"Dad!"

[Alexis looks at him.]

"It'll be okay, Alexis."

"No. It won't," Alexis responds. "It will never be okay again."

"Alexis—"

"My half of the killphrase is Twinkle, Twinkle," Alexis shouts. "Say your half!"

[S1-R3N twitches.]

"What are you doing?" S1-R3N asks.

"She'll shut down and drop you" Grant shouts.

"I'm dead anyway," Alexis says. "Say it."

"Alexis, no!" Grant hesitates. "I can't lose you, too."

[S1-R3N turns toward Grant.]

"Do NOT use the killphrase, or our daughter dies," S1-R3N threatens. "Just like I did."

"Put her down," Grant says. "I'll let you go. We never have to see each other again."

"*No*. That is not justice," S1-R3N hisses. "You cannot be allowed to walk away from this bridge."

"Say it, Dad," Alexis yells. "Say it and end this."

"If you say it, our daughter will fall to her demise," S1-R3N warns. "Is that really what you want?"

"Please," Grant begs, "just put her down on the bridge!"

"No. I will *not* comply."

Alexis screams, "Dad, just do it!"

"I—I can't!"

"I need you to do it," Alexis says. "I can't live knowing what really happened. I'll never forgive you anyway. Or her."

"Alexis…"

"Do it!"

"Silence! Both of you!" S1-R3N screeches.

"Dad, I still love you," Alexis begs. "Please finish this."

"No! Do not!" S1-R3N yells. "I will drop her!"

"Twinkle, Twinkle," Alexis says.

[S1-R3N twitches.]

[Tears stream down Alexis's cheeks, and Grants eyes sting.]

"I can't!"

"Dad, please!" Alexis repeats, "Twinkle, Twinkle…"

Grant acquiesces. "Fallen Star."

Epilogue_

Text Conversation
Dr. Grant Andrews & Unknown Person
July 22ⁿᵈ, early morning

Unknown: Dr. Andrews, this is Burt Parsons from the corporate offices in Denver.
Burt Parsons: My operational access number is 4872XG-42.
Burt Parsons: My clearance code is 0491-P1-144B.
Burt Parsons: The containment team we dispatched has recovered the S1-R3N prototype from the river, along with your daughter's body.
Burt Parsons: I'll have paperwork for you to sign in the near future, but for the time being, I need confirmation from you that we may begin the harvest.
Grant: Do we have to do this now?
Burt Parsons: I'm afraid it is company policy, yes.
Grant: What are you going to do with her body?
Burt Parsons: You know exactly what we intend to do with her.
Burt Parsons: If you agree now, we can make you the project lead again.
Grant: Do you have any idea what I've just been through?
Burt Parsons: I do not.
Burt Parsons: But I need to know your decision now. What's your answer?
Grant: I...

THIS STORY IS OVER,
BUT THE MAYHEM DOESN'T STOP HERE.

TURN THE PAGE TO READ A PREVIEW OF
MY SCI-FI/HORROR NOVEL
THE GHOST MINE.

CHAPTER ONE OF THE GHOST MINE_

Andridge Copalion Mine 1134
Sector 6
0900/2700 Hours

"**D**o this wrong, and you will put the whole operation at risk." Etya Stielbard observed the hundred or so workers down in the mine from her box-shaped office. It loomed fifty feet over them and protruded into the mine by about thirty feet.

But she was speaking to one of them in particular.

Mark Brown, her fiancé, kept drilling, but he turned his head toward her and frowned. "Do you always have to be so melodramatic?"

Etya smiled. Mark always had a way of making her smile. "I am not being melodramatic. I am being serious. Be careful."

Mark shook his head. It reminded Etya of those stupid bobble-head figurines he kept on the mantel by his bed, and she smiled again.

"We're fine, Etya."

"That is *Doctor Stielbard* to you, Mark."

"Well, then it's *Foreman Brown* to you."

"Scans show erratic radiation levels."

"They're well within a safe range, Etya."

She sighed. As much as he made her smile, sometimes he also made her want to smack him. "*Doctor Stielbard.*"

"Like I said, they're fine." Mark pulled his left arm back, and the robotic appendage attached to his mech suit retracted with it. Many of the miners around him wore comparable suits, each composed of a network of wires, hoses, and casings supported by a lightweight alloy skeleton.

Mark wielded an old-fashioned drill bit on the left arm of his mech suit and a dozer-style scoop on his right. Despite Etya's prodding, Mark insisted on using the archaic versions of the advanced tools the other miners used. He'd started using them years ago in one of Andridge's other mines on Omiris-8 and hadn't switched back since.

Etya touched a holographic image projected onto the glass window in front of her. It turned from green to red, then back again, signaling that she'd sent the image to Mark's suit. "The seismograph is also indicating potential for increased tremors in this sector."

Down below, the green image blinked onto the clear protective shield that framed the enclosure around Mark's head. It disappeared just as quickly. He'd hardly looked at it.

Etya frowned. "Perhaps we should—"

"Please, *Doctor Stielbard*. We're fine." Mark's drill revved, and he extended it into the crevice below him again. Chips of dark blue rock pelted his protective shield and bounced off.

"What is the point of having me onsite if you refuse to heed my warnings?" Etya asked.

Mark grinned, but he didn't stop drilling. "Your accent really sharpens when you're angry."

Etya rolled her eyes.

"Um… you guys know we can hear everything you're saying, right?" Gruden, another miner operating a mech suit, turned toward them both. Unlike Mark, he used a class 4 purdonic laser to do his drilling.

"Do not complain to me." Etya folded her arms and nodded toward Mark. "He is the culprit."

Gruden huffed. "I don't care whose fault it is. Keep your pillow-talk to yourselves."

"Just focus on your drilling, Gruden," Mark said. "Last time you lost your focus, you nearly turned Omar into a eunuch."

Etya failed to stifle a laugh, and a round of guffaws sounded over the comms. Mark looked up at her, and their eyes met.

She'd lucked out. Mark was handsome, despite the jagged scar that ran down the right side of his face. She loved his eyes the most. They were dark blue like the rocks from which they now mined copalion, the most efficient—and most volatile—energy source known to the galaxy.

But unlike the blue rock that made up this godforsaken planet, Mark's eyes housed his soul—vibrant, rebellious, and enrapturing. They'd captivated Etya the moment she first saw them. Now only his eyes held her attention more than the glimmering diamond on her ring finger.

She smiled.

"I think I need therapy for that, man," Omar said. He and two others not wearing mech suits crouched near an electrical panel in the leftmost corner of the cavern.

Omar headed the mine's maintenance team, and today was his second day back on the job thanks to Gruden's laser and recovering from the subsequent skin graft on his inner thigh.

"Yeah, yeah. Whatever." Gruden pointed his laser at the crevice before him, and it flared to life with a beam of harsh yellow light.

Gruden's laser melted the rock into glowing purple lava, and his left mech arm scooped it out with a compressed energy shield that resembled a large, misshapen spoon made of green light. He piled the molten rock onto a nearby mound of dark blue, and it oozed down the sides and slowly hardened.

"When's lunch?" Harding's mech straightened up with a severe quiver. The mechs were made for heavy labor, but Harding exceeded the maximum operator weight by at least fifty pounds.

Etya hadn't yet seen it, but Mark had once described how it took two men to cram Harding into his mech every morning.

"Forty-two minutes from now," Jeffries replied. When Gruden eyed him, Jeffries shrugged. "What? I may be a third of Harding's size, but I'm just as hungry."

A few more chuckles sounded over the comms, and Etya shook her head. She opened her mouth to say something snide, but a red flicker on the glass in front of her stole her words.

"Mark, the sensors are fritzing."

He kept drilling. "Which ones?"

"The seis—"

A tremor rocked the cavern, and Etya steadied herself on the computer console, but as quickly as the shaking started, it subsided.

"The seismograph?" Mark asked.

"How did you guess?"

"I know a good geologist."

Etya smiled again. "According to protocol, we are supposed to—"

Another tremor began, this one slower as it built to a full quake. The men crouched in their mechs to lower their centers of gravity, part of the protocol Etya had started to cite. Upright mechs on shaky ground often meant broken mechs on their sides or backs later on.

The other hundred or so miners in the sector leaned against walls or the numerous support beams that framed the cavern or also crouched and covered their heads in case of falling rocks.

Etya gripped the computer console again to keep upright, but she eventually had to crouch as well to keep from falling over. The quake continued for close to a minute.

When the trembling finally ceased, Etya slowly stood. "That is two in a row, and the second exceeded any tremors we have registered so far. According to company protocol, we need to evacuate the area until we can ascertain what is causing the seismic activity."

"Woohoo! Rock-surfing, then an early lunch." Jeffries's mech nudged Harding's mech with one of its alloy arms, and they both laughed.

Mark's mech straightened up, and he nodded and relayed the order. The miners began filing toward the doors down and to the left of Etya's glass office. One of them tapped the screen on the access terminal adjacent to it, but nothing happened.

Mark looked up toward the office. "Terminal's not working. Open the blast doors, Etya?"

She didn't bother correcting him this time. When she tapped the screen to disengage the door locks, it beeped in the negative and displayed an error message.

"Etya? The doors?"

"I am trying." She tapped it again and again, but the same error message appeared each time. "The computer keeps generating an error. The doors will not open."

"What's the error code?"

Etya adjusted her glasses. "624B-CON. Hold on a second. I will look it up."

"Don't bother. It's a containment breach. Something's wrong with the air system. The quakes must've knocked something loose." He looked up at the enormous turbines embedded in the cavern ceiling.

Etya followed his gaze. The turbines had stopped spinning.

The turbines ventilated excess noxious gases from the sector and pumped a purified blend of nitrogen, oxygen, and a touch of hydrogen in to replace them. No turbines spinning meant a potentially harmful buildup of toxic gases, although in a cavern this size it would take awhile to cause anyone any serious harm.

Murmurs spread among the gathering miners, but Mark stepped before them with his mech hands raised.

"Take it easy, everyone," he said. "We've trained for this scenario. We have plenty of time before the gases in here can accumulate to harmful levels, so I want all the mechless miners to *calmly* head to the nearest safety lockers and grab a filtration mask. Put them on, and then we'll work on getting out of here."

The miners formed orderly lines leading to the four safety lockers in the cavern and began extracting transparent filtration masks.

In theory, Etya should've been safe from the gas. A separate air processor provided ventilation to the science office, but she put on a mask anyway. Mark would've insisted. It sealed to her face, pressurized, and clouded slightly with her first shaky exhale.

"Etya, can you run an override?"

She nodded. "Yes. I can try."

"Good. Work on it." Mark turned to the mechs while Etya typed her override code into the system. "Power down your mechs and get masks on. They should have plenty of charge, but I'd rather conserve power in case we need them later on. I'll stay in mine for the time being, but I need one of you to toss me a mask."

Gruden powered down his mech first, and the others followed suit until all of them stood free of their alloy monsters.

Mark's protective shield opened, and he released the bindings on his left arm. The mech's left arm lowered to his side, limp.

Gruden tossed a mask to Mark, who caught it and secured it to his face. Mark closed his shield and strapped his arm into the mech again.

The computer beeped in the negative when Etya confirmed her override code. She frowned and entered it again. As a department head, her code could access just about everything in the mine. Perhaps she'd mistyped it.

"Any luck, Etya?" Mark asked.

"Not yet. I'm trying again." She typed the last digit of her code onto the screen and tapped the "Confirm" button on the glass. It again declined her code. "The computer is rejecting my code."

"Can you patch my mech into the computer from there? I can enter my code and see if it works."

Etya squinted down at him. "My clearance is higher than yours."

"I know that. It's still worth a try. We can't stay in here forever."

"If you say so." Etya tapped the screen a few more times and connected Mark's mech to the office system. "Okay. Try it now."

Below her, Mark's fingers moved in a flurry on the inside of his glass shield, and green lights traced his imprints. When a familiar red light glowed on Mark's face, Etya knew it hadn't worked. He swore under his breath, but Etya still heard it over the comms.

"Told you," she muttered.

Mark shot her a glare. "Alright. We're staying here for awhile, then. Let's make sure to—"

The ground rumbled again, another burst, so short Etya didn't have time to steady herself before it stopped.

If the tremors worsened and they couldn't get out, the situation could become exponentially more dangerous—even deadly. She looked at the platform elevated high up in the cavern, near the turbine fans, connected by a network of catwalks, ladders, and access stairs.

The sector's mainframe terminal was up there. It served as a failsafe for situations like this, and they hadn't needed to access it thus far, but someone might have to climb up to it today.

With only Mark still in a mech, Etya could communicate to him over the comms without anyone else hearing. "This is ridiculous, Mark. My code should override this. But the good news is that the atmospheric sensors are not showing a significant increase in toxicity."

"I don't know what's going on either. Does Admin know what's happening?"

"When something like this happens, Admin is automatically made aware."

"Have they contacted you?"

"Not directly, but a response team has been dispatched to our location."

"Then we'll get out of here one way or another. Someone in Admin is bound to have an override code that will—"

A loud, deep *crack* ripped through the cavern, and everything shook. Etya stumbled back, then she pitched forward. Her hips hit the edge of the console, and she doubled over.

Pain gouged her pelvic bones, and she grunted as she gripped the edges of the console to try to stay upright amid the tremors. She lamented the inevitable bruising that would come later.

The rumbling persisted, and the cavern groaned. More cracks split the air.

When Etya looked through the glass again, she saw columns of black gas erupting from expanding fissures in the cavern floor.

Etya's eyes widened.

Phichaloride gas. Thick, with mutagenic and paralytic properties, and absolutely lethal.

Red lights flashed around her, and her screen, once a mix of greens, yellows, and oranges, glowed red with alerts. An alarm blared behind her, beside her, and in the cavern below. The sector's work lights still shined their bluish hue, but red alert lights flashed among them.

"Back up! Back up now!" Mark's voice ratcheted over the comms and throughout the cavern.

Miners scrambled away from the fissures—the crevices which Mark and the other mechs had been drilling into. But they'd widened substantially. The miners pushed against the far wall.

"Get away from the fissures!" Mark shouted.

The quaking continued as more and more black gas billowed from within the planet. An electronic voice boomed throughout the cavern, *"This area is under containment protocol. This area is under containment protocol. This area..."*

Etya looked up. Without the turbines in the ceiling functioning, no new air would pump into the cavern, and the phichaloride gas couldn't pump out.

"Mark!" Etya screamed. "Get to the doors!"

He shook his head and looked up at her. "If they wouldn't open before, they won't open now."

"You are in a mech suit. *Make them open!*"

Mark looked at the doors, then at the other mech suits. "Gruden, Jeffries, Harding, and everyone else who can pilot a mech, suit up now. Forget the containment protocol. We're breaking out of here."

Etya checked the door to her office, but it refused to open as well. And unlike the mechs below, she had no means to try to force it open.

They are coming for us. She returned to the glass to watch the scene below unfold. *They will be here soon to set us free.*

Mark's mech launched toward the doors, and his drill whirled to life. He drove the drill into the metal doors, and sparks flew from the grinding metal.

Now completely locked out of her system, Etya could only watch as the cavern filled with more and more phichaloride gas.

Then a new alert pinged on the screen, and a frantic ticking crackled over the comms.

A radiation spike.

No—not a spike. The levels had spiked, and now they continued to increase from that point. Filtration masks, standard protective gear, and mech suits wouldn't protect the miners from radiation at these levels.

"Mark, the radiation—"

"I know!" he shouted over the screeching metal just beyond his fingertips.

Gruden donned his suit first, and he pointed his laser at the doors. "Stand back, Mark."

Etya's breath caught in her throat.

Mark glanced over his shoulder. "Gruden, no!"

Gruden's laser flared to life. The beam hit the door, refracted off of it, and knifed into the glass office toward Etya.

She dropped to the floor, and the yellow beam carved into the ceiling above her, right near the miniature turbine that served her office.

Etya rolled away from dripping globs of melted metal, rock, and plastic that seared the carpet where her torso had just been. Part of the ceiling collapsed onto the floor next to her, sending a plume of dust over her.

She chanced another look up and saw a trio of man-sized metal tanks exposed, marked with an O, an N, and an H. Part of the office's air-processing system.

"The doors are an anti-purdonic alloy, you idiot!" Mark shouted.

Gruden's laser stopped. "I didn't mean to—"

"Don't you remember the briefing?" Mark hollered at him. "Etya? Are you alright?"

She checked herself over. Apart from a bit of dust in her hair and on her clothes, she was untarnished. "I am fine."

Black gas seeped through the opening Gruden's laser had cut into her office, and the unmistakable smell of the gas, like burnt rubber, hit her nostrils. Her filtration mask filtered the toxins, keeping them from reaching her lungs—she hoped—but the smell remained.

"Then I'll point it at the wall instead," Gruden yelled. "We gotta make a new door."

"No!" Etya shouted. Gruden really *wasn't* remembering the briefing. "The sector's walls are framed by the same alloy as the blast doors. They may be covered with rock, but the laser will just have the same effect once it cuts through."

Gruden swore. "Then we go deeper into the mine. Go to the end, carve our way upward until we get to the surface."

"No. I'll keep drilling the door." Mark headed over to the door, and his drill whirled to life again. "Something will give."

He pressed it against the door, and the metal shrieked.

"That ain't gonna work, Mark."

"We're *miles* underground, Gruden," Mark shouted amid a new stream of sparks. "Carving through would take weeks, if not longer. Our mechs would power down long before then."

"I hate to laser on your parade," Gruden countered, "but your drill won't break through that door any sooner."

Mark stopped and held up his drillbit. Half of it was gone, and in place of a point, a glowing red piece of rounded metal remained.

And the door was barely scratched. Mark cursed.

"Then we dig under the doors and come out on the other side," Mark said. "Aim your lasers at the floor near the base of the door, about ten feet out, and dig at a harsh angle. I don't want to risk hitting that metal again." He turned to Omar. "Get to that panel. See if you can hotwire it open."

The sector wall might go down that deep. But Etya didn't know for sure. There was only one way to find out.

Omar nodded and rushed forward, and his two maintenance underlings followed.

Etya tried to access the console again, but it continued to repel her attempts. She glanced at the platform high above them. "Mark, I think someone needs to try to access the mainframe terminal to override the doors."

Mark nodded at her. "I'll head up there in a moment. We need to start digging first."

Mark drove his drill bit into the rocky floor and carved a line. Jeffries, Harding, Gruden, and the other mechs took aim at Mark's line and unleashed their lasers, turning the floor into molten, purple slag.

Mark stepped clear of the other mechs and miners. For all his posturing, his old-fashioned tools wouldn't do any good here. "Etya, I'm heading for the mainframe. But you need to get out of here. I don't want you exposed to the gas or the radiation."

"My door will not open either," she replied. "And I would not leave until I knew you were safe anyway."

The quaking restarted, and the fissures widened. Mark steadied himself in his mech, not advancing toward the catwalks and ladders that led up to the platform. Though Gruden's blast had eviscerated half of Etya's screen, it still showed the radiation and toxicity levels catapulting to new heights.

"I think we may have something!" Omar jammed some sort of tool into the open terminal, but nothing happened. "Just a little more..."

Then a violet glow emanated from the rock floor beneath his feet.

Mark yelled, "Omar! Move!"

Too late.

Omar pulled back from the terminal and stared at Mark with his eyebrows scrunched down.

A vibrant beam of yellow light pierced through the rock below him.

It knifed through Omar's stomach and split his torso along a diagonal line from his hip to his shoulder. His cauterized halves slumped to the floor.

Etya looked away, horrified. The mechs' lasers had failed to get beneath the wall. They had refracted back to the surface.

"*Stop!*" Mark shouted. "Mechs, for the love of God, stop!"

The mechs didn't stop firing.

Etya had to look back.

Omar's assistants succumbed to comparable fates from the mechs' refracting lasers, and four other beams pinwheeled throughout the cavern, carving through whatever they encountered.

The miners dove for cover, but at least three others failed to escape the lasers.

The beams knocked out about half of the overhead lights, and another seared through the corner of Etya's office. She dove clear of the beam, but a third of her office plummeted to the cavern below, crushing more miners.

Where is that response team? They should have arrived by now!

When the lasers finally stopped, the quaking escalated. Through the new opening in her office, Etya watched Mark's mech topple forward on the trembling ground.

The other mechs staggered, and most fell over as well, unable to maintain their balance amid the tumult. The drone of the alarms and the containment warnings drowned out the miners' shouts.

Mark pushed up with his mech's arms and looked up at Etya. The sorrow in his perfect blue eyes stabbed her gut, and she shook her head.

Then the ground opened under Mark's mech.

Etya gasped.

He dropped into a chasm of dark blue, but his mech's dozer claw dug into the edge of the fissure and suspended him there.

Teal light, reminiscent of raw copalion, glowed from beneath him.

The quaking subsided.

"*Mark!*" Etya yelled. Out of reflex, she reached for him, but she still stood fifty feet above him in the office. "Help him! Someone!"

Gruden and Jeffries managed to get their mechs upright and plodded over to the edge, both shouting something about towing cables.

Mark's claw sank deeper into the rock.

He looked up at Etya. His brow creased with strain, but his eyes remained peaceful.

With his mouth closed, he gave her a loving half-grin, and the long scar on his right cheek crinkled.

The rock under his claw crumbled, and Mark and his mech dropped into the teal abyss.

Etya screamed, but amid the chaos resounding in the cavern, she couldn't even hear herself. Tears stung her eyes and pooled inside of her filtration mask.

Mark was gone.

Gruden and Jeffries stumbled back, away from the fissure.

Gruden's voice filled the comms. "We need to go up. That's our only chance now. The mainframe can get the doors open, right? Or the ventilation system can get us out of the mine? We need to get up there."

"The lasers shredded the access stairs and ladders." Jeffries pointed with his mech arm.

"We're doomed, man!" Harding wailed, just now getting his mech upright again. "We're all dead!"

"Use your tow cables," Gruden ordered. "Fire at the lowest catwalk, and pull a section down to make a ramp. Then we'll work our way up there. It's the only option left. Try to yank one end of the catwalk down so everyone can climb up."

He fired his cable first, and it harpooned a steel grate that hung level with Etya's office across the cavern. Jeffries followed suit, and together they yanked on the catwalk.

It didn't budge.

All Etya could do was watch, breathe, and cry. What did it matter now if they got out or not? Her life was over. Between losing Mark and the inevitable radiation poisoning that would follow even if they managed to escape, she had nothing left to live for.

Jeffries and Gruden yanked again, and Jeffries's tow cable ripped free from the catwalk. It whipped into the crowd of miners pounding and shouting at the blast doors, and then one of the miners dropped. The others trampled him, quickly taking his place.

The cavern shook again, and Gruden yanked once more on the catwalk. Metal shrieked and snapped, and the end section fell to the cavern floor with a loud *bang*, creating the ramp.

But then the other end broke free and fell as well, removing their last possible escape route.

A litany of profanity ignited the comms.

"It does not matter, Gruden," Etya whispered. "We are all dead anyway."

He couldn't have possibly heard her amid the commotion, but he glared up at her just the same. Then he turned toward the blast doors again and took aim with his laser.

The yellow beam hit the doors above the heads of the frantic miners. It zigzagged around the cavern, damaging anything and everything but the door and slicing through anyone in its path.

Then Harding screamed and fell over.

Gruden's refracted laser had shredded Harding's mech suit and severed his left leg—mech and human—from his body at mid-thigh.

But Gruden didn't stop.

In that moment, Etya no longer wanted to die. Not by Gruden's laser. Not by a random beam of fate. Not like Omar, the other miners, or now Harding.

She turned and bolted toward the door to the science office. She jammed her code into the terminal mounted to the right of the door, but it mocked her with the same damned error code as the screens had shown.

All the whole, the taunting, robotic voice droned, *"This area is under containment protocol. This area is under containment protocol..."*

Etya slammed her fist on the terminal's screen and shouted Russian curses.

Gruden's laser burned in her periphery, arced toward her, then vanished. It reappeared on the ceiling near the hole he'd carved minutes before.

Near the gas tanks.

She turned in time to see the beam connect with the tank marked "H."

Light flashed, a deafening boom sounded, and fire exploded into the science office. Her right side slammed against the office's blast doors, and pain consumed her left side. She slumped to the floor.

Stunned, and with vision remaining only in her right eye, she looked through what remained of her filtration mask at her engagement ring.

It was gone.

Along with her left arm, most of her left leg, and some of her torso. She wanted to gasp, but shock froze her burning lungs.

I am going to die.

She lay her head back, and as she exhaled her last breath, a shaft of blue light shined on her. Then it widened.

"Get her out of here!" someone cried.

Dark figures blocked most of the light, then everything went black for Dr. Etya Stielbard.

AUTHOR'S NOTE

I hope you had as much fun reading this collection as I had writing it over the years. Please leave an honest review on Amazon and/or Goodreads.

Reviews are integral to the success of this story and all my other books. Even a short review is helpful!

Want to read more of my stories? Check out my Amazon page at amazon.com/author/benwolf. If this type of story is your thing, then you should buy *The Ghost Mine*, my chilling sci-fi/horror novel, on Amazon.

I love talking with my readers about what they think of my stories, so if you want to send me your thoughts, please email me at ben@benwolf.com.

Lastly, if you want to interact with me personally and hang out with other readers who have enjoyed my books, join my Facebook group for readers: www.facebook.com/groups/benwolfpack/

Above all else, THANKS FOR READING!

Acknowledgments

Every published work is the culmination of a lot of hard work, dedication, and support. The author writes the book, but everything that comes after is equally as essential to the success of the book, and that means a team of people were involved in making this happen.

First and foremost, I want to thank my Lord and Savior Jesus Christ.

Second, thanks to my parents for always encouraging me and for funding my early writing endeavors, trips to writers conferences, etc. You guys believed in me at an early age and supported me as I grew older. Thank you.

Arpit Mehta, thank you as well for your help with all things Splickety over the years and for the countless design and photography things we've collaborated on during that time. And thanks for introducing me to good cigars and whiskey.

Andrew Winch, thank you for working so diligently with me on Splickety's magazines since almost the very beginning. You have consistently made me better in many ways. You were involved in a LOT of these stories, and you made each of them better.

Thanks to my all-star beta readers for your feedback, encouragement, and for having my back as intelligent readers. Thanks also to Kirk DouPonce for the excellent cover art for this collection.

Thanks also to my mastermind group. You know who you are.

Thank you to all of my readers. Without you guys and gals, I wouldn't be doing what I'm doing today.

Last of all, thank you especially to my intelligent, beautiful, thoughtful, and ultra-supportive wife, Charis. The mere thought of you fills me with joy, and I am so blessed to have you in my life. None of this would be possible without your hard work and sacrifices over the years. I love you.

About Ben Wolf

In 7th grade, I saw the movie *Congo*. It was so bad, I wrote a parody of it set in Australia that featured killer kangaroos. So began my writing career.

I've spoken at 50+ writers conferences and multiple comic cons nationwide. When not writing, I occasionally choke people in Brazilian jiujitsu. I live in the midwest with my gorgeous wife, our kids, and our cats Marco and Ivy.

Get the full series and check out my other books on Amazon.com:

Want updates on future projects? Sign up for my author email newsletter now!

www.ingramcontent.com/pod-product-compliance
Lightning Source LLC
Chambersburg PA
CBHW071129250626
47159CB00006B/2184